Law and Disorder: Moving Violations

An Ellora's Cave Publication, July 2004

Ellora's Cave Publishing, Inc.

PO Box 787

Hudson, OH 44236-0787

ISBN #1-84360-950-9

ISBN MS Reader (LIT) ISBN #1-84360-637-2

Other available formats (no ISBNs are assigned):

Adobe (PDF), Rocketbook (RB), Mobipocket (PRC) & HTML

Edited by KARI BERTON

Cover art by SCOTT CARPENTER.

LAW AND DISORDER: MOVING VIOLATIONS

By

LORA LEIGH *and* **VERONICA CHADWICK**

Chapter One

Jericho, Tennessee. The hick town still held so many bittersweet memories. Rebecca Taylor had only visited once since she'd left and she wouldn't be back now if Aunt Josie hadn't died. Rebecca frowned as she searched the cabinet for more plates. The house was full of people. Some she knew from her childhood, some she didn't know. Rebecca had few memories of her father's reclusive sister, but she knew she didn't have friends. She hardly ever left her house. Aunt Josie had been such a private woman. Rebecca never expected this many people would attend her funeral, much less come by the house to offer condolences.

She walked into the dining room and set the plates at the end of the highly polished mahogany table, looking it over. Covered dishes, casseroles and cakes were plentiful and there was one lone bucket of Kentucky Fried Chicken. She couldn't help but smile at that. The doorbell rang and Rebecca sighed. At least maybe with all these people all the food would be eaten. She'd hate to have to throw it away.

Rebecca made her way through the crowd occasionally nodding and saying, "Thank you," as folks laid sympathetic hands on her arm and whispered their condolences.

Finally she reached the door, swung it open and looked up into the face of Jackson Montgomery, her first love. It didn't matter that he was ten years older than her. It didn't matter that he'd only seen her as a pesky little kid. Even when she was sixteen and her dad brought her along that summer to check on Aunt Josie.

He had been a Marine then, home on leave, and she had fancied herself in love. Her young body was blossoming and hormones were raging. She had flirted shamelessly and he'd teased her as usual. Still, it had been a powerful crush and the memories of those emotions had stayed with her through the years.

At the tender age of eleven her parents had yanked her roots and moved away from her quiet country hometown to the cold, often cruel city of Detroit. She'd been torn away from the only life she'd known, from friends she'd had since birth and grown up with, people she cared about and who cared about her. It had been painful for her, but what especially broke her young heart was leaving Jackson.

Now here he was again and that familiar tug low in her tummy was still there. He looked amazing in his black slacks and dark gray dress shirt. He took off his black Stetson and thick black hair fell across his forehead in spite of the good cut. There wasn't an inch of fat on that flat stomach. He had broader shoulders, leaner hips, and well-formed thighs with new bulges in all the right places. Rebecca let her eyes travel to his mouth and couldn't help but admire the way his full, well-defined lips contrasted with the hard planes and angles of his tan face.

Jackson had definitely changed; he'd gone from cute and sexy to hot and dangerous! "Jackson," she said with more composure than she felt. She mentally shook herself and stepped back from the door.

He stepped in, shutting the door behind him, never taking his intense gray eyes from hers. "I'm sorry I couldn't make it to the funeral but I wanted to come by to extend my condolences."

She couldn't find her voice so she just nodded and smiled tremulously.

He stepped closer and rubbed her bare upper arm. "How are ya holdin' up, Pixie?" His hand was warm, a little callused, and sent a sizzling electric current through her body. She crossed her arms over her chest to hopefully hide her tightening nipples. God, could he see what he did to her?

"I'm okay, Jackson, thank you," she croaked then cleared her throat. "Everyone brought food. The dining room table is overflowing. Help yourself."

He followed her through the living room to the dining room. She turned and almost jumped back. He was standing inches away looking down at her. His brows furrowed, his gaze sharply assessing her. She could smell him—warm, spicy male. She felt flushed with heat, awareness. She opened her mouth to say something but forgot what she wanted to say.

"Are you sure you're all right?" Jackson asked, softly tilting his head.

Damn, he was gorgeous. *Okay, Rebecca, get a hold of your libido.* "I'm fine, really."

Jackson smiled and little lines at the corners of his eyes fanned out, giving him a sexy air of mischief. "Sit down and talk to me for a while," he said as he sat and pulled out the chair beside him. "I haven't seen you in what? Ten years?"

Rebecca nodded and sat, thankful to be off her shaky legs.

"I'm really sorry about Josie," he said gently, compassion clear in his eyes.

"Me too." She smiled sadly. "I really didn't know her, Jackson. All these people knew her better than her own niece. I regret that."

Jackson shook his head. "These people didn't know Josie, Becca, any better than you did. That's the way Josie was, she liked her solitude."

Rebecca frowned and gestured toward a blue-haired woman sitting on the couch sobbing, clutching another woman's hand. "Mrs. Holt is devastated."

"Becca, Irene Holt never even met Josie. She attends any and all funerals and wails and carries on like that at every one of 'em." He narrowed his eyes and gave her a lopsided smile.

Rebecca's eyes widened and she tried not to laugh. "No way."

"Yep." Jackson grinned. "As for the rest of them, they're just being neighborly. Most of 'em still remember your family and you. You were pretty hard to forget with your 'pixie pest' ways. They're fond of you and wanted to be helpful, show they care."

"That's pretty incredible," she said, looking around at the quiet gathering. She looked back at Jackson, meeting his gaze. "What about you?"

"Oh yeah, they're fond of me too." He waggled his brows.

"Ha, ha." Rebecca narrowed her eyes.

Jackson's smile faded and his eyes darkened as he held her gaze. "I was always fond of you, Pixie. You were a great kid, even if you were a little pest that was constantly drooling over me and giving my girlfriends hell."

She had been such a little tomboy with wild young girl fantasies of being swept off her feet by the cutest boy in Jericho, or the whole wide world, for that matter. He'd called her his Pixie Pest and tugged at her long tangled hair and still made her young untried heart pound in her chest. Much like it was now. Only her heart wasn't untried anymore and she knew what that liquid pull low in her stomach meant.

"I'm not a kid anymore," she said without looking away.

Jackson's gaze traveled over her body. "I've noticed. I'm trying really hard to remember what a pain in the ass you used to be."

Rebecca lifted a brow. "I can still be a pain in the ass, Jackson."

"Hmm. I bet you can." He met her gaze again and held it. Her eyes dropped to his mouth. She wondered what those gorgeous lips would feel like on hers, on her breasts, on her stomach… For as long as she could remember she'd wanted Jackson to look at her like he was looking at her now. But he was making her feel way too hot, way too needy. She didn't need anyone. And after Todd Lawrence, the very last thing she needed was another relationship.

She stood. "I'm being rude sitting here. I better go mingle. Eat something." She needed to break the heavy silence that hung between them. He gave her a lopsided smile, took the plate and continued to watch her as he stood.

"Uh, there's iced tea in the kitchen, make yourself at home." She turned, took a deep breath and walked into the living room.

Time plodded along as Rebecca sat in the dim little living room with its floral prints and crocheted doilies. She listened and nodded and thanked those who stopped by. They asked about her parents and patted her hand sympathetically when she explained that her father had died three years ago of a heart attack. Their concern for her seemed genuine and the kind words and gentle touches were a surprising comfort to her. She found herself remembering her childhood and that rare country hospitality she'd missed for fifteen years.

It was late when the last person, none other than Mrs. Holt herself, hugged her, patted her cheek and left. Rebecca shut the door and leaned against it, shutting her eyes with a sigh. It warmed her heart that these people, regardless of their motives, not only spent time cooking for her, but also gave up their entire Saturday for her. It made her feel she'd been cheated.

"Everyone finally leave?" Jackson watched her with those observant silvery eyes of his.

He stood there with that lopsided smile and his hands in his pockets, looking like he'd just stepped out of GQ. Erotic images flooded her imagination and every cell in her body stood to attention. Endorphins flooded her system and sent that erotic heat washing over her body. Her cunt clenched, liquid arousal pooled between her sensitive lips, dampening her panties. Damn, it had been too long since she'd been touched.

"It appears so." She pushed away from the door. "Everyone except you."

Jackson watched her. Something in his eyes made her heart leap. She swallowed and gestured toward the dining room. "You should take some of that food home."

Jackson shook his head. "Already put up. There wasn't much left but it's in the freezer, labeled, dated and everything. Dishes are all washed and put up too."

"Wow." Rebecca smiled. Okay, he was looking way too perfect. "Thanks, Jackson."

"No problem. You're tired; you didn't need to have to face the mess." He stepped closer. "There's a plate for you in the fridge. Do I need to stay and make sure you eat it?"

She smiled up at him. If he stayed any longer she'd rape him for sure. "No, I'll eat it, I promise."

It annoyed her that she was disappointed that he wasn't going to try and take advantage of her. Her life was so up in the air. She knew she didn't need the entanglement but she wanted the warmth, the affection. She could feel the heat radiating from his body and she struggled not to lean into him.

"When are you going home?" His voice felt like a caress and she nearly whimpered.

"In the morning," she said breathlessly

"Are you selling the house?" he asked quietly.

She sighed and furrowed her brows. "I don't know yet. I had planned on it, but now…I don't know."

He watched her for a moment. "It was good to see you again, Pixie." He touched her face gently then took her into his arms. "Don't stay away so long next time."

She wrapped her arms around his back and resisted running them over the hard planes and over his round, tight ass. His body was hard and hot against hers. Her breasts felt heavy and swollen, her hardening nipples ached. She cringed knowing he could probably feel them pressing against his chest and pulled away, swallowing hard. "No, I won't."

He pressed his lips to her forehead then met her gaze. She watched in fascination as they darkened and turned stormy. She opened her mouth to say something and he lowered his head and kissed her mouth. A small kiss, lingering only seconds, but the impact was powerful. She looked up at him with wide eyes. He let her go and she felt suddenly cold.

"Be careful going home," he said hoarsely.

She nodded, folding her arms over her chest.

He turned and opened the door. "If you need anything let me know." He walked out onto the porch. "Lock up."

"I will." She fought her desire to ask him to stay.

"Goodnight, Becca," he murmured.

"Goodnight, Jackson." He pulled the door shut and she chained and bolted it. Rebecca walked into the spotless kitchen, her body humming with arousal. She ran her fingers through her hair in frustration. Sleep was definitely going to be hard to achieve tonight.

Chapter Two

Jackson left the house, his blood boiling and pooling in his loins, his cock rising hard and hot between his thighs. Damn, Becca was even more beautiful now than she had been years ago. The sixteen-year-old had been an emerging woman, more tempting than she could have known. But now, more beautiful than ever, she would be more than he could refuse.

He shook his head as he jumped in his truck and turned the ignition. He almost hadn't shown up at the house. Had avoided the funeral and the showing like a plague. He had known Becca was there, and had known she would be as tempting as she always had been.

Slipping the vehicle in gear, he pulled quickly away from the curb and headed home. Good thing she was leaving tomorrow. Distractions like Becca were more than he needed right now. His uncle's death six months ago had left the sheriff's position to him until the next election, and Jackson still hadn't solved the riddle of his uncle's murder. And he knew damned good and well it was murder.

His last conversation with Tobias Montgomery, the tough, ex-Marine turned sheriff who had helped raise him, played through his mind.

"Something's up, son," he had told Jackson quietly as they sat on the porch of the Tobias family home. "That mayor's dirty dealin'. I can smell it."

He had spit a stream of tobacco juice off the side of the porch before leaning back in his chair. Tobias had been in his fifties, robust and healthy, and as agile-minded as he had been in the Marines.

"How so?" Jackson had watched him curiously.

He had known Mayor Whittaker all his life. The man was a sleaze ball, but he had never been an illegal sleaze ball.

Tobias had shaken his gray head slowly. "Not sure," he had grunted. "But I'm tellin' you, Jackson, I know him. He's flashing money he shouldn't have, and meeting with some real slick characters of late. He's edgy, and his wife's death was too suspicious to suit me. That was a fine woman he was married to."

Tobias' voice had been somber. Margaret Whittaker had been Tobias' girl before she married the other man. When Tobias had joined the Marines and went off to Vietnam, she had married the only son of the caretaker rather than waiting for him to return. Tobias had never gotten over it, as far as Jackson knew.

Jackson had wondered at the time if his uncle's affection for the deceased woman hadn't had something to do with his suspicions concerning the mayor. Now, Jackson wasn't so sure. Tobias' sudden "hunting" accident just didn't ring true, especially considering the fact that Tobias wasn't a hunter. A fisherman, a bullshitter, but not a hunter.

Like any proud southern boy, he had his hunting rifles, he shot trap when the occasion called for it, but he didn't hunt. "Won't eat it, I ain't killin' it," had been his reasoning. Now he was dead. The official report being that he had tripped, causing his rifle to go off and blow a hole in his chest. By the time Jackson had gotten home the body had been cremated and any chance of another coroner's exam shot to hell. And Jackson was left to figure out what the hell had happened and why. He was no closer now than he had been six months ago.

He pulled into the sheriff's office and sat in the gathering darkness, staring at the aging stone building that housed the jail, as well as his office. He didn't trust his men or the mayor. And the few friends he had grown up with were mostly gone now. Not that he was an outsider, except in the sheriff's department.

There, he was feeling more and more alone amid the few deputies who seemed much too friendly with Whittaker.

All but Bryan. Bryan Matthews had been Jackson's only addition to the force. He wouldn't be there if it hadn't been for Jackson's brother-in-law.

"Hire the boy," Ted had suggested quietly after Jackson had taken office. "He's dependable and needs the experience." At the time, Jackson had been aware of the general atmosphere of insubordination that he was facing.

He could fire them, he knew. Roby and Martin, the two deputies causing him the most concern. But it would be harder to keep track of them that way. They were involved, but how he wasn't certain, and he needed to know how.

It wasn't adding up. The influx of drugs into the county was no more than a few peddlers from larger cities that were weeded out on a regular basis. There weren't many strangers in town, and few unusual occurrences unless you counted the short disappearances Whittaker made. Where the hell he went, Jackson had yet to figure out.

He shifted in the truck, frowning in irritation as his throbbing cock reminded him of Becca once again. Dammit. He doubted very seriously she would ever return now that her aunt was dead. Despite her indecision over keeping the house, she was a city girl. He could see it all over her. Damned fine city girl. But a city girl, all the same.

He drew in a deep breath, willing his stubborn hard-on to return to a relaxed state. Hell, maybe he had been too long without a woman, but one-night stands weren't his thing, and now wasn't the time for a relationship. It would be fine, he thought. Damned fine to curl up with Becca, hear her moaning in passion, her slender body undulating beneath his.

"Dammit," he growled, his hand clenching on the steering wheel as his cock seemed to harden further.

"Hey, Sheriff," Bryan hailed him as he caught sight of the truck after leaving the sheriff's building. "Sure is a pretty night, huh?"

The kid was too damned green, Jackson thought.

"Evenin', Bryan. It's a fine night," he agreed as he pulled the keys from the ignition and got out of the vehicle. "You off for the night?"

"Yep. Calling it a night," Bryan nodded as he pushed his blond hair back from his forehead and stopped on the sidewalk as Jackson approached. "I thought I might drive out to the lake. There's a few friends meeting up there tonight."

Bryan shifted from one foot to the other as though standing still was too much for his body to handle. He was like a pup, always ready to dive into the next adventure.

"Be careful. Give me a call if anything starts looking rough. Don't play Superman. You're not made of steel," Jackson warned him.

Bryan grimaced. "You're as bad as that danged brother-in-law of yours. I'm not stupid either, Sheriff."

There was a shade of offense in the kid's tone. Jackson sighed. Damned kids didn't know the dangers that existed out there.

"I'm aware of that, Bryan." He nodded. "Just a warning I'd give to any of my men. No offense intended."

"Yeah. Okay then. I'll be careful," Bryan promised. "Sorry, Sheriff."

"No apology needed. Night, Bryan." Jackson moved off then, heading for the double doors.

"Hey, Sheriff," Bryan called out again, his voice pitched low now, questioning.

Jackson turned back to him, seeing the hesitation on Bryan's face.

"What is it?"

Bryan scratched his head, frowned, and glanced around the area as though making certain they were alone. "I heard something strange today."

Jackson waited patiently as Bryan stepped nearer.

"Roby got a call, and whoever he was talking to got pissed enough to start yelling. I was standing there…" Bryan grimaced. "I feel like a tattletale. I'm sure it's nothing, but the man was cursing him loud enough to wake the dead. I couldn't help but overhear."

"And?" Jackson stiffened as tension invaded his body.

Bryan shook his head again. "And it was just damned strange. Could have swore the words were Arabic, ya know? Or something similar. When did we get foreigners in town?"

Jackson shrugged, fighting a sense of excitement. "Hell, who knows who Roby has pissed off this week."

Bryan chuckled. "Hell if that ain't the truth. I figured it was nothing, but you know, after the Towers…" Bryan sobered.

"Yeah. I know." Jackson nodded. "Go have fun, Bryan. You know Roby. He keeps everyone pissed."

"Yeah, guess so." But Bryan sounded as uncertain as Jackson felt. "I better go then."

Jackson watched as Bryan turned and headed to the parking lot. He searched the area carefully, his eyes narrowing as he assured himself no one had overheard the conversation. It might be nothing, as he had tried to convince Bryan, but it wasn't the first clue he had come across. Now, he just had to figure out what the hell it meant.

Chapter Three

Rebecca's return to Detroit had been nothing short of depressing. She'd grown tired of the brutality of the big city. Being a cop, she'd seen it all. The slower pace of a small town police force was very appealing and being back home reminded her she was a country girl at heart. So, she had looked into a transfer.

She chuckled remembering the wild and crazy girl she used to be and shook her head. She'd been such a tomboy. With her skinned knees and wild mop of hair and freckles. She was forever running all over the county getting into mischief. She had such great memories of fishing in the lake, swimming in the deep part of the creek, climbing trees, falling out of trees.

The move from Jericho to Detroit had been a major drama as was everything in Rebecca's young life. At the time it felt as if her heart had been snatched right out of her chest. And then there was Jackson. Seeing him again when she was sixteen had been the clincher. That fine lookin' man had sent her painfully immature heart to pounding like mad all over again. Silly girl, she thought, fancying herself in love with a twenty-six-year-old man at such a young age. But she wasn't a silly girl anymore, and Jackson was still around.

Pushing the thought aside, she mentally listed the things she still needed to get done before reporting to the station the next morning. Finding her PDA topped the list. She was hoping to try and reach the sheriff's office this evening, but the number was on that blasted device, as was most of her semi-organized life, and it had conveniently disappeared. Breathing out roughly, she scanned the scattered contents of her purse on the table and frowned. So, she hadn't lost it in the bottom of the "pit" after all. That didn't leave many other places to search for it.

She had tried to get in touch with the sheriff a couple of times before she left Detroit and a few times since she arrived in Jericho but he was always out. She'd left three messages but he'd never returned her call. Ah, well, maybe she would get lucky when she went into the station the next morning, she thought with a heavy sigh. Someone there would be able to get all the preliminary crap taken care of and get her orientated. If not, then she would just have to figure it out for herself. Not a pleasant thought, but not anything she couldn't handle.

She wasn't going to worry about it. She was starting a new life, and that deserved a small celebration. The idea hit her like a flash of inspiration. That was it! She was gonna visit the Wild Rose Tavern and maybe run into some old friends and Rita, if she was still there, couldn't fuss at her this time! At the tender age of eleven she'd been determined to sneak into a bar, no less, hoping to get a glimpse of Jackson. Pixie Pest, he'd called her and tugged at her long tangled hair, right before Rita would kick her out and call her mom. She sighed as the thought occurred to her…wasn't that what she was doing tonight? Hoping to catch a glimpse of Jackson? Damn.

She stepped into the steamy shower. She couldn't believe he was still there. Since he had joined the military like his daddy wanted him to, she had thought he would be overseas or at least stationed far away from home. She'd heard that he'd been in Special Forces and that he was assigned exciting and dangerous missions. It only added to his appeal. She'd prayed for him while he was fighting in Desert Storm.

Well, if by some chance he was at the Wild Rose, she thought as she rubbed the rich foamy lather over her body, she'd have to keep her distance. Jackson could never live up to her fantasies and the last thing she needed was a one-night stand. She stood with her eyes closed, letting the warm spray rinse away the suds.

She stepped out of the shower into the small humid bathroom, wrapping a towel around her. She wiped a washcloth across the mirror then carefully applied a little makeup and blow-dried her hair. She tilted her head, giving herself a quick check in the mirror, then went into the bedroom and dressed. She'd arrived in the small rural town just that morning and already she looked like the hick she was in her denim sleeveless button up shirt, shorts and leather thong sandals. It amazed her how easy it was to slip back into it, how comfortable she felt. She wouldn't dream of going out to a bar dressed like this back in Detroit.

She would have worn her midnight blue slip dress with the rhinestone spaghetti straps and her silver heels. She would have spent a couple of hours at the salon having it pinned up in some elaborate configuration. She frowned at herself, trying to picture what she'd look like with a chic short cut. May not be a bad idea, she thought. The severe bun she wore while at work made her scalp ache. It felt good to have the unruly golden brown hair loose and hanging free past her shoulders in wide thick curls.

Her lips tilted. Yes, this was much more comfortable, except for the bra, but she didn't think that her C-cup bouncy boobs moving freely under her shirt would go as unnoticed here as it did in Detroit. But then, in Detroit she'd be going to a dance club, where there would be House music at its worst and brightly colored strobes and erotic sounding drinks, like Orgasm and Sex On The Beach.

Instead, she was going to the Wild Rose Tavern where they would be playing country music at its best. There'd be line dancing and beer. Besides, she might see some of her daddy's old buddies. That would just be weird. This was definitely a change for her. She wondered if anyone would recognize her as she painted her lips with hot pink, cherry flavored lip-gloss and dropped the tube in her little leather bag. Then checking to make sure the clip was full, she dropped in her weapon also.

* * * * *

Rebecca handed the man sitting at the door her money and ignored his toothy grin and roaming eyes. She decided against sitting at the bar and made her way to the small table in the dark corner in back. She sat there a moment, looking for familiar faces. Her body began to move to the music, when an older woman in a halter-top and jeans sashayed up to the table. Her hair was aggressively teased and piled on top of her head like blonde cotton candy, the prettiness of her brown eyes was lost in the heavy black mascara caking her lashes. "What'll ya have, hon?" she asked around her gum. It was all Rebecca could do to keep from gaping. She hadn't seen Rita in years and she looked just the same. A couple of wrinkles here and there, but still the same.

"Rita!"

"Yeah?" Rita asked defensively then looked down at Rebecca, narrowing her eyes. "Hey, I know you, you're…ah…" Rebecca couldn't help the grin that spread across her face. Rita frowned, tilting her head to the side as she tapped her pen against her chin, thinking back.

A large hand rested on Rita's shoulder. "That there is the Pixie Pest herself, Rita."

Rita's warm brown eyes widened in surprise. Her bright red lips spread into a grin. "Little Rebecca? You better get up here and give me a hug!"

Rebecca jumped up and embraced the woman. Over Rita's shoulder, Rebecca's gaze locked with those familiar silvery gray eyes that glinted with humor. A slow smile slid across her face. Damn, he was hot. The dark blue shirt he wore opened at the neck and tucked into his tight black jeans. His sleeves were rolled up, revealing muscular forearms. In one strong hand he held two frosty bottles of beer.

Rita held Rebecca away from her and shook her head. "Just look at you. All grown up." She glanced back at Jackson then rolled her eyes. "Oh boy! Well, I guess I can't kick your smart-mouthed little ass out this time. So have a good time but stay out of trouble, you hear? I can still call your momma," she said, grinning. Rita patted her cheek. "It's so good to see ya, hon. Holler if ya'll need anything."

"Will do," Jackson said and Rita shot him a look as she walked away.

"Have a seat." Rebecca gestured to the booth across from her. He sat as he slid the bottle across the table to her.

"Thanks," she said keeping her eyes on him as she took a pull from the bottle. Those old butterflies were coming to life in her tummy.

He was leaning forward watching her. "I saw you come in. It's good to see you again."

Rebecca rolled her lips inward to hide her grin. In a million years she would never have imagined she'd be sitting across from Jackson Montgomery in the Wild Rose drinking a beer. "It's nice to be here…legally."

He nodded and grinned. "You here for a while this time or just tying up loose ends with Josie's estate?" He continued to watch her with those sexy eyes of his. They were always so expressive, so warm, and so full of mischief.

Was it her imagination or was there a challenge in those molten silver eyes? She narrowed her eyes and smirked. "I think I'll be here a while."

"Good. We can catch up. We didn't really get to talk much when you were here for Josie's funeral." Those sexy lips tilted at the corner. She nearly moaned as she imagined how they might taste.

"That's true. It was a short and busy visit. But it was good to see everyone again. I missed Jericho more than I realized." She took another pull of her beer and tried to regain her composure. What was it about him that one look from him melted her and had her body aching for his touch?

"So, did you miss me?" He lifted a brow and watched her closely.

Rebecca shrugged. "Nah, haven't really thought about you." Liar, she yelled at herself. Jackson had always been her hottest wet dream.

"You really haven't changed all that much." Jackson smiled. Damn, even his smile was hot.

"I haven't?" Rebecca frowned.

"Well, you've brushed your hair." They both laughed. "And you've filled out."

"What?" She scowled at him.

"You know what I mean, you've grown..." He looked pointedly at her cleavage, lingering there, and cleared his throat. "...in all the right places."

"Nah, Jackson, I'm just a 'pixie pest', remember?"

"Oh yeah," he grinned. "I remember, you drove me nuts. You know, Lana still hasn't recovered from the time you dumped a whole can of worms on her head at the lake."

"Good," Rebecca snarled. "I never liked her. Oh Lord, you didn't marry her, did you?"

"Hell no! I didn't like her all that much either, but she was easy, Becca, and I was young and had outa control hormones." He took a long pull from his beer.

Rebecca nodded slowly watching his throat work, feeling her body heat. "Outa control hormones. And thwarted by a lovesick eleven-year-old. Tsk,tsk tsk."

"Yeah." He caught her gaze and held it as he laid his open palm on the table in invitation. "Do you still love me, Becca?"

She tilted her head and arched a brow as she put her hand in his. "Aw, Jackson, I had to move on. I couldn't wait around pining after you."

He held her hand, his thumb making suggestive circles between her thumb and first finger. Rebecca wondered how in the world the icy bottle of beer stayed cold in his hands when she felt suddenly flushed at his touch. She and Todd had broken up almost a year ago and even before that, Todd had never been all that attentive. Now this man she'd always fantasized about was awakening her desire. It had been dormant way too long.

He put his free hand over his heart. "Oh man, my little Pixie Pest broke my heart." He leaned closer. "I always thought you'd wait for me, Becca."

She gave him an exaggerated look of sorrowful repentance and patted his hand with hers. "Did you ever quit your lover boy ways and get married, Jackson?"

"Nope. Never found anyone who measured up to you." He looked at her with a hooded gaze, clasped her hand and pressed it to his lips.

Rebecca felt that kiss all the way to her toes. She rolled her eyes and snorted. "Did you ever really believe you could?"

"Nah, not really." He grinned. Sexy little laugh lines fanned out from the corner of his eyes. Her eyes were drawn to his lips and she groaned inwardly. "How 'bout you? Did you find someone after you quit pining over me?"

Rebecca thought of Todd Lawrence and cringed. "Almost, but not quite. I escaped just in time." Boy, was that a true statement.

Jackson watched her. His voice lowered, vibrating through her. Her nipples responded, straining against the thin fabric of the bra cups holding them. "I always liked you, you know. You were always a pretty little thing. Too bad you were a baby and a royal pain in the ass."

She squeezed his hand. "You are so full of it, Jackson Montgomery. You're just trying to get in my pants 'cause I ain't a baby anymore..." She hoped, anyway. She leaned closer and whispered, "...and 'cause I grew boobies." Even now those "boobies" were aching for those strong hands, that gorgeous mouth.

His laugh was deep and rich, it rumbled low in her stomach and sent delightful shivers all over her body. "I'm wounded. I've grown, Becca. I've changed."

"Have you?" Rebecca shifted in the booth as she felt the moisture gathering between her thighs. She felt overheated and overwhelmed.

"Uh huh." He let his gaze wander lower again. "But damn, girl, you do have great boobies."

She watched him, still amazed that she was sitting here with him and that he so obviously wanted her. She allowed a small, wicked smile to touch her lips. Here was her chance. She wondered just how brave she really was. He looked decidedly ready. Definitely interested. Rebecca wasn't a one-night stand kinda girl but if it turned out to be just that, would it be worth it? After all, she'd only wanted this man her whole adult life. But was she bold enough to make the first move? From the darkening glint in his eye, she had the distinct feeling she wouldn't be rejected.

She bit her lip and slipped her foot out of her sandal, keeping her gaze on his. His eyes widened as she gently caressed his inner thigh till her foot connected with the cool plastic of the booth seat. His lips tilted at the corner as he reached under the table. His long fingers began massaging her foot, applying just the right pressure at just the right places. Rebecca felt the touch radiate all the way up to her crotch. He was making her so wet with just the slow seductive pressure he applied to her foot. What could he do to other places?

When his hand moved to the top of her foot and then to her ankle, she slowly inched forward. She could feel the heat before she felt the bulge. Jackson narrowed his eyes and she couldn't help but grin. Her foot trailed up and down his thickening erection, pressing against the denim. He was long and thick and very hard. Lowering her eyes she measured him in relation to her foot and nearly gasped. Oh yeah, just like in her dreams. What do you think of your Pixie Pest now? Uh huh, she grew the hell up, she thought.

"*Unzip your jeans,*" she mouthed. She watched his eyes darken. His hand stilled on her leg, then he moved to his pants to do her bidding. She bit her bottom lip as she carefully moved her foot inside his jeans and massaged the length of his hard hot cock through his underwear with her toes. She knew her daring exceeded even her limits. She didn't know what emboldened her. There had always been something about this man. Maybe it was the unmistakable arousal in those steel gray eyes that made her brave now. It could be her years of fantasy, the very real heat growing between her thighs, or her sudden desire to make this cowboy beg. God knows there'd been nights she begged for him.

Rebecca watched Jackson's Adam's apple bob as he swallowed hard. Her lips parted and she licked her dry lips as her toes trailed slowly, lightly up and down his hot shaft again and again. She watched him silently, lifted the beer to her lips and drank. She lowered the bottle only far enough to run her tongue around the rim, watching his eyes follow every move she made. He breathed in hard, his lashes lowering. One strong hand gripped her foot, quite effectively halting the torment he was enduring. He clumsily adjusted himself and zipped up.

"Let's dance," he said, his voice hoarse, heavy with arousal.

She barely had enough time to slide her foot back into her sandal before he was pulling her toward the dance floor. "I don't know any line dances."

"S'okay, it's a slow song," he answered hoarsely.

He yanked her against his hard body and she closed her eyes and breathed in the scent of him. God, she needed this.

He held her close for a long time, his hand splayed on her lower back. His little finger was doing slow magical things against the top cleft of her ass.

"Do you know what you're getting yourself into here?" he whispered against her cheek.

She felt her cunt clench and pulse with the moisture of her arousal as she moved against him. She nuzzled his neck then licked and sucked it. He tasted even better than she'd dreamed. "Yes, Jackson, I'm not a little girl anymore," she breathed.

His breathing quickened. He lowered his head and cupped her face, kissing her hard. His tongue tasted like beer and lust.

She gently sucked on it and swallowed his groan. She imagined the feel of that talented tongue rasping against the sensitive inner folds of her cunt, and her body trembled against him in reaction. He trailed kisses along her jawbone and nibbled her earlobe.

"I want to make you come," he whispered harshly.

"I want you to make me come," she whispered back.

His big body tensed, his hands clenching at her hips as he ground his erection against her. "Let's go." His breath was a harsh rasp against her ear.

"Lead the way." She let him grip her hand as he pulled her through the smoky bar.

Outside, the air was thick and hot and just added to her sexual irritation. "You wanna go to my place?"

"I'll follow you." He leaned down and kissed her deeply, pressing his body to hers. Her hands moved up his chest and he pulled away. "Be careful, but be quick."

Chapter Four

Her emotions were rioting as she pulled into the drive of her small house and stepped out of her car. She heard Jackson shut his truck door behind her and her hands shook in anticipation as she tried to find the key. Jackson's arm snaked around her middle, and pulled her back against him as he took the key from her.

His heat infused her, melting her to the core as he devoured her neck with his mouth. Her breath hitched, her legs were like rubber, and she felt consumed with lust. She would have fallen through the door if he had not held her so tightly against his solid body.

They hurried through the door and he shut it behind them. She turned in his arms, his mouth found hers and she thought she would go up in flames. Those wonderfully firm lips moved over hers, sending ripples of pleasure through her. His tongue slid between her lips, sensually caressing the warm interior of her mouth.

His hands slid down her back to cup her ass. It felt so good, so incredibly good. She'd never felt need like this. Any hesitancy disappeared; apprehension gave way as he ground his straining erection against her. Her pussy throbbed as her cream soaked her panties. She moaned, taking his lower lip gently between her teeth. "Jackson," she gasped against his mouth letting her tongue soothe the bite. Her hands combed through his hair.

"Bedroom," he growled, his mouth moving over her jaw to her ear. She didn't bother with the lights as she led him through the small living room down the hall to the bedroom.

In the bedroom he pulled her into his arms again. He kissed her hard, possessively, sending desire spiraling through her. He managed to unfasten her shorts, pushing them quickly over her hips as she fought to free her legs. He smoothed his hand over her butt and up her back and she trembled at his urgent touch. She pressed hungrily against him, wanting him closer, to feel him inside her, stretching her. His hands were just rough enough, just hot enough to make every inch of her throb with need.

He walked her backwards till her legs hit the bed and she felt herself falling. His hand molded and massaged her breast as he kissed and nibbled along her collarbone. A shaky breath escaped her lips on a moan as his mouth left a burning trail down her breastbone and he quickly unbuttoned her blouse.

Her shirt lay open and he opened the front hook of her bra with a flip of his wrist. Pushing the flimsy material aside his hand cupped one breast while his mouth caressed the other. Her body shuddered with need and the walls of her vagina convulsed. Finally, his mouth found one nipple as his fingers found the other.

He sucked, nibbled and kissed, torturing her slowly. He squeezed it lightly between his lips, flicking it with his tongue until she moaned and arched against him craving more of the exquisite ache. "Such beautiful breasts, such nice juicy nipples. Mmm," he murmured against her ultra sensitive skin. That gorgeous male mouth was definitely well versed in the female body.

"Oh please, Jackson, I'm on fire," she whimpered, fisting her hands in his shirt and pulling it free of his pants. He was driving her wild. Little tremors gripped her with every pull of his mouth on her nipple, every flick of his tongue made her want to scream.

She unfastened his jeans, pushing them down and freeing his expansive cock. She was on the edge of a climax from what he was doing with his mouth alone. She struggled for breath as the sensations coiled inside her tighter and tighter. Her fingers bit into his well-shaped ass, loving the feel of his hard muscle flexing under smooth skin.

"Now," she begged. Reaching between them she trailed her fingers over his silky, steel-hard shaft before wrapping them around it. She felt the blood pump into his thick flesh as she urged him forward. She had waited so long, fantasized about him moving inside her. She needed him now.

"Not yet, baby, not yet." His hands restrained her, his big body controlling her effortlessly as she urged him to completion.

She whimpered. Her body trembled with the intense sensations coursing through her as he continued to trail kisses down her body, his tongue torturing her. "Yes, now!" she said breathlessly as she writhed beneath him. "Oh God, please, Jackson."

He circled her navel with his tongue. Heat speared though her as he bit the tender flesh there, sucked it then soothed it with slow, moist strokes. His hands moved up and down her inner thighs spreading her wide. He moved lower and lower until he was kissing, gently nibbling the top of her cunt.

His tongue stroked over her soft tender lips, slid between her moistened cleft then laved her heated flesh with long and firm upward strokes. She was so close, so close. Jackson's lips closed over her clit and sucked hard. Her breath caught in her lungs and she bucked up as she climaxed hard and fast. He gripped her hips, lapping up her juices as she thrust against him with each crashing wave of her orgasm.

Jackson rose above her as she slid bonelessly back to earth. She was breathless, gasping, and despite the release, she wanted more. Her body hummed, throbbed, she still wanted him inside her. He quickly stripped his shirt off as he moved up her body. Without giving her time to fully recover he slowly slid his fingers into her, the walls of her vagina gripping them as it pulsed with the aftershocks of her orgasm. Then he slid them up through the slick folds of her flesh, driving her up again as he found the firm rippled flesh of her G-spot. He took her nipple into his mouth, nibbling, flicking his tongue over it, making it harden further and she pushed forward for more. God, someone should patent his fucking tongue, she thought as she groaned with growing need.

She ran her hands up his muscled back and fisted them in his hair. She was frantic for him, wanting to consume him. She pulled him up to her and kissed his mouth. Her hands moved down his stomach and caressed his balls, letting her fingers trail up his steel-hard, thick shaft. He pulled away from her and met her gaze. His eyes had gone dark and heavy-lidded. Her thumb rubbed across the tip of his cock and smoothed the drop of pre-cum around the hot, smooth head.

"You've got a wonderful cock." The deep, hoarse whisper surprised her, made her feel sexy. She licked her swollen lips. "I want to feel it in my mouth."

"God, you know how to tease a man." He moved his fingers inside her and gently pressed his thumb against her clit. "Later, if you still want to. Right now I want to feel your tight cunt snug around my cock." She inhaled sharply as the sensation shot through her, pushing her upward. He moved his hand from her and positioned himself over her. Moving the full head of his thick shaft through her slickness, up and down through her swollen folds. He rubbed slow circles around her clit. She clutched at his shoulders.

"You're so good," she moaned as she felt him push into her. He took her arms and lifted them over her head and leaned down and kissed her, sucking her bottom lip. He moved deeper into her, stretching her further. She was on fire. Rockets were exploding in her body, her blood racing through her veins. She had never felt this. Never known this. Never even dreamed it would be this hot, this mind shattering. It was the worst form of torture she could imagine and it felt so damned good. She felt the sensations building…she was almost there, almost ready to come. She fought against it, wanting it to never end.

He rose, lifting her thighs and he draped each ankle over his shoulders. He grabbed a pillow and braced it under her as he grasped her hips and filled her to the hilt. She cried out harshly, arching into the strong thrust. She clenched her muscles around his cock and he closed his eyes, hissing air through his teeth.

"Slow, baby, slow," he groaned. He slowly withdrew till he was almost free then plunged back in.

"No, faster. I want it faster," she cried out in desperation. She needed it. God, she was dying here, and all he wanted to do was tease her.

"Relax, Rebecca, trust me." His voice was rough and deep, dark and sexy.

Rebecca moaned harshly, panting, wanting to scream at him to just fucking hurry.

He kissed the inside of her ankle while he began pumping in and out of her in a slow rhythmic motion. Waves of sensation washed over her like honey. She wasn't used to going slow. It was driving her up, higher and higher, the sensations becoming sharper and sharper until she thought she'd go mad. She looked up at him and met his gaze. He looked hungry. She ran her hand down his hard rippling stomach to where their bodies met. She closed her eyes and tilted her head back as her fingers felt his hot cock slide in and out of her, felt his balls slap against her.

His hand closed over hers and she opened her eyes again, watching him as he directed her fingers to the little swollen nub nestled in the slick folds of her female flesh. He was thrusting into her faster and faster. She sucked in a breath as his finger and hers rubbed over her clit, taking her up until she exploded, shards of sensation radiating through her. She cried out and flung her head back. Jackson drove into her, still rubbing and tenderly pulling at her clit. She bucked against him as the next orgasm hit, even stronger, until she thought she'd splinter and disintegrate. His lips parted on a groan and his eyes narrowed, focusing on hers, plunging into her one last time as he came and shuddered against her, his hot cum filling her.

She lay panting as he lowered her legs and lay on top of her, his semi-hard flesh still seated inside her. It felt good to have the weight of this man on her, better than any of her fantasies.

She had this irksome fear that no one else would ever measure up.

Chapter Five

Jackson figured he was screwed, and not just literally, as he rolled to his side, bringing Rebecca's body close against his chest. Damn, if that hadn't been the best fuck of his life. The fiery heat and melting passion he found in her was more than amazing, it was downright scary. No woman should be so tight, so hot and wet, her inner muscles sucking every drop of semen from his taut balls until he was gasping.

This was his Pixie Pest. He remembered the gangly little girl that had followed him so many years ago, hero worship shining in her eyes. She wasn't a little girl any more, though. She was a full-grown woman, and he'd be damned if she wasn't like a flame in his arms. And she still made him feel like a hero. He couldn't believe how hot and hard that made him now. From the moment her eyes had stared into his at that damned bar, he had been ready to explode. It wasn't normal, he warned himself almost fatalistically.

And even now, he was semi-hard; his sensitive flesh achingly aware of the slick, hot portal awaiting it inches away. He could feel the smooth satin of her thigh against the sensitive head of his cock. He knew within minutes he would be hard and ready again. Dammit, he didn't need this. All he wanted was a good time, a few beers, a dance or two, and if he got lucky some hot sweaty sex. He hadn't expected a wildcat that sapped his strength and made him want to howl at the moon in male satisfaction.

She was resting against him, her breathing slowly evening out, the perspiration drying on her skin. Shower. That's all he needed to clear his head, he thought. A shower. He could get up right now, and walk right out that door. Hell, his house wasn't far away, and the water was nice and cold there. He knew that for a fact.

He shifted to move away from her. He had everything figured out until his betraying flesh slid across slick, silky flesh. He closed his eyes on a groan and settled between her thighs once again instead. Okay, so the cold shower could wait.

He rubbed his face against her full, hard-tipped breasts. They were gorgeous. Round and firm, with little pink nipples that tempted him as surely as anything could. Like pretty raspberries, all prime and ripe and ready to pluck. His tongue stroked one softly.

"Again?" There was surprise in her voice. That crisp, stern Yankee accent was shocked, but growing husky with the return of heat.

Who would have thought his Pixie Pest would return with that upright starch in her voice that made her sound so damned untouchable? It made his libido stand up and howl in hunger.

"This is the South, sugar," he whispered with a smile, allowing his country twang to deepen to a slow drawl. "We aim to do it right."

"I believe you did it pretty damn right the first time," she gasped, as his lips pulled at one little berry with a teasing caressing.

"I'm sure I can improve." He smiled against her flesh.

"Improve?" Her sexy green-gold eyes widened incredulously and she bit her plump lower lip. "God help me," she murmured, her longs fingers fisting in the sheets at her sides as she arched her head back against the pillow, pushing her breasts closer to his mouth.

Damn, she was responsive. Her breath hitched, suspended, then released on a low moan of pleasure as he transferred his attention to her other nipple.

"Oh, that feels good." She seemed surprised as he drew on just the tight bud of nerves tempting his lips and tongue. He went no further. He just touched her nipple, laving it, worrying it gently between his teeth, listening to the strangled gasps that issued from her throat.

"Someone was in a hurry earlier," he teased her as he kissed the darkening flesh. "We take things slow here, darlin'. Nice and easy, so we can savor every experience. Remember?"

She arched languidly in his arms, a small, whimpering moan escaping her lips as his tongue rasped over her again, then he drew her nipple into his mouth, suckling at it slow and easy. The hard little point throbbed beneath his lips, tightening and stabbing at his tongue in needy greed.

"This is savoring?" she asked in breathless amazement. "God, Jackson, this is torture."

But she struggled to lie still beneath him, her hands gripping his shoulders as he sipped and sucked at her breasts, loving the taste of the berry firmness as she arched against him.

"Torture?" he asked her gently, smiling when her little nails bit into the tough skin of his upper arms, and her thighs shifted against his, her hips grinding against the thigh he pressed to her hot center. Damn, the woman was like fire in his arms. Like pure lava, melting and flowing from her core, dampening his thigh with a liquid plea.

"Jackson, I don't know if I can stand this," she panted harshly, her hands reaching to spear into his hair as he licked from her nipple to her neck.

His let his teeth rasp the sensitive skin at her collar bone, then lick at it with a slow swipe as he tasted the smooth sweetness to be found there. She tossed her head, groaning as he pressed his thigh against her drenched mound, allowing her to ride it as her hips rose and fell in demand. Unable to resist that long lovely neck flushed with heat from her arousal, his mouth devoured her, sucking and licking the warm silky skin of her throat. His hand caressed her breast, gently lifting, molding, squeezing, rasping her hard nipple against his palm. He felt the rumble of her groan against his tongue, and his mouth moved higher, along her jaw.

"Of course you can, sugar," he whispered, his tongue outlining her ear with a slow sweep.

He raised his head and found her mouth open, soft and yielding. He tasted that full, hot, lower lip she kept nibbling on and drew it into his mouth. He tilted his head and deepened the kiss, their breath blending as he moved his tongue against hers in long slow strokes.

He felt her shiver against him, and his cock throbbed in its own demand. Damn, where had his self-control gone? She made him want to thrust hard and deep and drown in the heat pouring from her. He had to force himself to let his hand move slow and sure from her waist to her breast. There, he cupped the mound of heaving flesh, moving his head to rub the hard little nipple against his cheek.

She cried out harshly, her hot cunt thrusting quick and hard on his thigh as he pushed it harder against her. And still he didn't hurry. He wanted her to remember this night, just as he knew he would. He rubbed his lips over the hard little point, licked it tenderly, then moved back to her neck as one hand moved lower along her smooth, flat abdomen. His fingers trailed through the beads of moisture forming there. Her skin was almost as slick as the hot folds of the flesh between her thighs. And he wasn't unaffected either. He could feel the sweat pouring from his body, drenching them both as he fought for breath.

He moved then, drawing his thigh back from the heat of her cunt as he spread her legs wide, moving between them slowly.

"Jackson, please." She shivered, whimpering in her female need as he nudged the slick entrance of her body with the broad head of his cock.

Control. He fought for it. He didn't want to slam inside her. He wanted it to last forever. He wanted to take her gentle and sweet, and show her how damned good it could be. He slid in marginally, barely an inch, feeling her muscles clamp onto that small invasion in desperation.

He fought for breath. Son of a bitch, it was good. So damned hot and silky, clenching, stroking his flesh with each harsh breath she fought for. He moved both hands to her hips, holding her steady, his eyes moving to the point where their two bodies met. The dim light of the moon's glow spilling onto the bed gave him a clear view of her glistening, silky curls, and the burrowing of his hard length between them.

He swallowed tightly, on fire with the sensations sweeping through his body as he inched farther inside her, his eyes riveted by the sight of her female lips widening, drawing him in as the suckling motions of her vagina kept his cock pulsing with the need to climax.

He wasn't going to rush this. Damned if it wasn't the best he had ever known. Watching her as he took her, seeing her body accept him, hearing her cries for more. He gave her more, spreading her inch by inch as her keening cry was lost in his male groan of triumph, as his darker, intimate hair meshed with her wet curls, soaking both.

He shook his head, grinding his hips into her as she screamed out for him to take her hard. Fast. But it wasn't his cock screaming out the demand, "Now, Jackson. Now." It was her tormented voice, a plea that shattered his self-control.

He fell forward, catching himself on his elbows and clasping her head in his hands.

"Open your eyes," he growled. "Look at me, Rebecca. Look at me while I make you scream."

His hips retreated. Her eyes widened in protest. He slammed forward, driving every hard desperate inch of his cock as deep as it would go inside the sucking depths of her vagina. Her mouth opened, a gasping cry issuing from it. Her pupils dilated in further pleasure, a harsh flush mounting her cheekbones as her hips pushed against him, demanding more.

"Faster. Please, Jackson. Faster." Her eyes didn't leave his; they glazed over, her eyelids lowering just enough to give her a mysterious, sexy look that made him crazy.

He felt his muscles bunch, braced himself with knees and elbows, and with a quick prayer that she would come quickly, he gave her what she wanted. What he needed. His hips powered into her. Thrust after long, hard thrust as they both groaned, arched, slamming their bodies into each other, fighting for the ultimate high as their blood thundered, rushed.

Rebecca screamed for him. He relished the sound, thrusting deeper inside her as he felt her clench, gush. Another sharp scream issued from her throat as she began to climax harshly. He was only a second away. He gritted his teeth, fought a shout, and lost his control as he felt the rippling power of his ejaculation tearing through his body.

"Becca!" He cried out her name, holding himself deep and tight within her as his seed pumped hard and fast inside her gripping, spasming flesh.

Damn, if he had to die, this was the way to go. Jackson barely caught himself before he collapsed on top of her. At the last second, he twisted his body, falling beside her, his eyes closing in exhaustion as he fought for breath, and for sanity. Yeah, that's what he needed. Sanity. Sex like this should be outlawed, though he'd hate to have to arrest himself.

He grinned at that. His hand fell to Rebecca's stomach, feeling the sharp rise and fall of it as she fought for her own breath. They were both gasping, fighting for control. He felt alternately proud as hell, and scared to his toenails. He wanted to beat on his chest, he wanted to slink away and hide from her. Sex shouldn't be that damned good.

"Amazing, you're absolutely amazing, but I think perhaps I've died." Her voice, so proper and well cultured, made him smile. Damn if he didn't have a bona fide Yankee. He'd never live it down.

Jericho, Tennessee didn't boast many Yankees. He was pretty damned sure they wouldn't brag about any, if they were there. And those who might be there hid it real well, to the best of his knowledge. But here he had a soft, vibrant, incredibly lusty she-cat on his hands, and he loved it.

"Sure 'bout that?" he whispered against her ear, feeling the involuntary shiver that raced over skin. "Just let me catch my breath, sugar, and we'll try for another round. See if I can bring you back to life."

Her breath caught. He heard it, felt the stillness of her body.

"Uh, slow down now, cowboy. Give a girl a moment to recharge," she said with a soft sexy laugh.

There was a faint protest there. Real faint, Jackson thought, wishing he had the strength for the chuckle he wanted to release. Damn, it was all he could do to breathe.

"Just rest there then." He took a deep breath, making himself rise and reach to the foot of the bed where the comforter had been tossed.

Damned A/C was hell on damp skin, he thought, feeling her shiver again. He covered them both, then settled back beside her with an exhausted sigh.

"I have to get up early." She cuddled into his arms, her head against his chest as a last sigh whispered over his chest. "Don't let me ignore the alarm."

He glanced over at the red digital display on her side of the bed. Alarm was set, at least. He would have hated to have to go to the trouble.

"Sure thing, sugar." He yawned, pulling her tighter in his arms, his chin resting against the top of her head as he closed his eyes.

Damn, a sudden thought struck him. She wasn't going to run him off before dawn? He frowned, wondering how long it had been since he had spent the night with a woman, instead of sneaking out of her house before daylight. Neighbors and gossip—they turned normally intelligent women into gibbering masses of nervousness. They wanted to play, but damned if they wanted anyone to know it.

He had always been amused by the same shy, sweet, parlor room ladies gasping and moaning in the dead of night, then pushing their lovers swiftly from the back door before dawn.

Not this one, though. He ran his hand along her back, finally allowing it to rest along the top of her buttock as he sighed in satisfaction. Maybe he'd try for more the next morning.

Chapter Six

Gary Allen's sultry voice had Rebecca smiling. She stirred from a warm dreamy sleep, opened one eye and groaned when she realized the singer's voice came from the radio that serenaded her awake and not the rugged sexy man himself...whose face kept morphing into Jackson's. Jackson... She opened the other eye and levered herself up on her elbows, wincing at the ache in her muscles. Her lips tilted a bit thinking of the previous night's activities.

With a heavy sigh she swung her legs over the edge of the bed to stand and walk through the house. Yep, he was gone. Now how the hell did he get up and out without waking her? She always slept so lightly. She frowned then shrugged and started a pot of coffee. Humming with the music from her radio, she walked back through her bedroom to the adjoining bathroom. She leaned over and turned the shower on hot, full blast, wrinkling her nose at the uncomfortable stickiness between her thighs.

Reality hit her. The Pixie Pest had hot wild sex with Jackson Montgomery. She'd gotten swept up in the fury of lust Jackson brought out in her, so fast. And oh, it was a fury. And here all this time she thought she knew what it was to have an orgasm. Since when did reality ever surpass fantasy? Since last night! Jackson definitely lived up to her wildest dreams. The memory of it washed over her with enough force to make her vaginal muscles clench in remembered pleasure.

She lathered her breasts thinking of him, those big sexy hands, those long clever fingers. Her nipples contracted, sending pulses of warm sensation through her. Her eyes drifted close on a shaky sigh. She let her soapy hands roam over her stomach, down her hips to her mound. She luxuriated in the silky lather she spread over her body in slow, languid strokes.

She slid her fingers over the tender flesh of her sore inner thighs. Waves of pleasure flooded through her. She moved under the hot spray and, tilting her head back, washed her hair. The water pounded over her, down her back, while she rubbed her hands over her breasts, the hard nipples rasping against her palms. She turned to feel the water beating down on her breasts, her distended nipples. Her other hand moved downward, dipping into the slick wet lips to the sensitive knot of nerve endings nestled there. She sucked in the thick steamy air though her teeth at the slow spiraling pleasure.

Her body reacted fiercely to the memory of Jackson's hands, his mouth moving over her body, as her hand moved over her clit. Her fingers delved into her pulsing channel and drew out the slick dew of her arousal. Her legs grew shaky and she stepped back, leaning against the cool tile. She imagined that Jackson spread her open, his three fingers that glided over the swollen, throbbing flesh.

She tormented herself with her hands and her memories, the sensation building and pulsing through her. She continued to rub, long firm strokes. Her lips parted, she felt the orgasm rising in waves till the climax peaked and tore through her. She tilted her head back, allowing the water to flow over her chest and down her body. Her hips rocked back and forth, her moans echoing off the tiled walls. She pressed her hand tighter against her slick flesh till the waves subsided, leaving her feeling relaxed, her muscles loose and liquid.

After she washed her hair and rinsed the last of the suds away, she reluctantly stepped out of the shower and wrapped a towel around herself. She needed to focus on the day and her new job. She wiped the steam from the mirror and started to brush her teeth when she noticed the love bite right above her left breast. A hickey, he'd given her a hickey. Good lord, she felt like a teenager again. She grinned, thankful her shirt would cover the mark. The smile stayed in place while she brushed her teeth and applied a bare minimum of makeup.

* * * * *

Rebecca pulled her Tracker into the small paved parking lot next to a monster sized pick-up truck—if you could call a truck that size a pick-up. She killed the engine and sat back to finish her coffee. They didn't expect her for twenty more minutes. She would feel much more comfortable if she at least knew the name of her new boss. For some reason it hadn't been in any of the transfer paperwork, the mayor hadn't mentioned it and she had forgotten to ask. She narrowed her eyes and gave herself a mental head slap. She hated not being completely informed, it put her at a disadvantage. However small, it was still a disadvantage.

Sheriff what's-his-name had been busy on the phone with the mayor when she called earlier and the officer she'd talked with hadn't seemed to expect her at all. On top of that, he didn't know if he had a uniform that would fit her or not. For today, her jeans and white cotton oxford shirt would have to do. She recalled the derisive humor in the officer's voice and got the feeling she was walking into a boy's club.

The police station building looked simple and a bit undersized, but someone took good care of the landscape. The tiny lawn was lush and green. The few meager hedges were neatly trimmed. She took a sip of her coffee and arched a brow. Maybe someone in there would remember her. If not, they'd just have to adjust, she thought.

She got out, grabbed her purse, laid a hand on the firearm at her hip and slammed the car door. She felt good, cocky, self-confident as she walked purposefully up the few steps. She took a deep breath as she swung open the door and looking up, froze in shock. She slowly took off her sunglasses and looked into those silver gray eyes that she watched go dark and stormy with a savage lust the night before. Her body shuddered involuntarily.

Jackson was slightly bent, checking some reports the officer sitting at the desk had evidently been typing. That wild sexy hair still fell across his forehead. His sensual mouth frowned at her. His shirt sleeves were rolled up, his snug jeans slung low on his hips. Gun and badge hung from his belt. Well, she probably didn't have to worry about somebody remembering her now.

Jackson cleared his throat. "Becca. May I help you?" His voice was deep and wary.

Careful to keep her face blank, Rebecca stepped forward and offered her hand. "Officer Rebecca Taylor. Your transfer from Detroit."

He straightened; she noted the muscle that pulsed in his jaw. His frown deepened as he stepped from around the desk and took her hand. Warm and calloused, it brought back that flood of erotic memories. She pulled away quicker than she should have. "Welcome home."

Her eyes widened and met his darkening gaze. *Damn, when she fucked up she fucked up good,* she thought. "So, you're the sheriff."

He stared, or glared at her, she couldn't decide. "I didn't know you were arriving till the mayor called this morning." His voice was deep and clipped. He was pissed. It showed in every hard line and muscle in his body.

"Oh." She shrugged, for the first time in her life at a loss for words. "Well, I…"

"He had tried to reach me last night," he interrupted her, pausing to let his gaze slide over her body like a lurid caress. "I was…unavailable."

She narrowed her eyes. Damn him, there was no need to bait her. If he wanted to make this difficult, by God, she could comply. "Well, I'm here now, Sheriff, so if we could just start this ball rolling." She motioned impatiently with her hand. "I'll fill out the necessary paperwork and you can have someone show me the ropes…"

"Follow me, Officer." Giving her no chance to defy him, he turned and walked briskly down a dimly lit hallway.

Was that a smirk? That jackass smirked at her! Oh, it was on now. She followed on his heels into his office and closed the door behind her. The room was small and plain. A few certificates hung on the white walls. A table with a Mr. Coffee sat beside a disheveled bookshelf. Two ugly gray-green file cabinets stood behind a wide wooden desk. A computer monitor sat among the many files, scraps of paper and post-it notes that littered the desktop, along with a fat coffee mug that said: *Sheriffs do it with handcuffs.* Rebecca resisted the urge to sneer.

"Jackson, this is obviously not a comfortable situation. If we'd known beforehand, last night would have…gone quite differently. But it can't be undone so let's just be adults about this and put it behind us, move forward, pretend it never happened." Easily said, she thought. Her body was heating up just being in the same room with him.

Jackson had walked around his desk and sat in his chair. He gestured to the chair across from him and she sat down. Leaning back, he propped his booted feet on his desk and folded his hands over his stomach. He pursed his lips as if to consider her suggestion then slowly shook his head. "Nah, ain't gonna happen. See, Becca, I saw the flash of heat in those sexy eyes of yours the moment you walked through the door. You can pretend all you want, darlin', but fact is…" He sighed. "You're hot for me. You always have been, you can't help yourself."

"Re-becca, not Becca," she hissed through her teeth. "I'll do my best to control myself." Now it was her turn to smirk.

"Yeah, but you won't succeed. We both know that, don't we?"

"Look, will you cut the snide remarks!" His smile looked more like a sneer and he nodded, at least it looked like a nod.

"Sheriff." She paused for emphasis and met his gaze. "I assure you, I have an excellent record and I play it by the book. You don't have to worry about me doing my job."

"I don't need you. I have all the officers I need. We don't have a whole lot of trouble here in Jericho." His gaze lowered to her breasts. She felt them stiffen involuntarily and had to struggle not to cross her arms. "No, I'm sure you're very, very good…at your job, Officer Ree-Becca."

His double meaning didn't go unnoticed. She wanted to slap that smug look from his gorgeous face. Damn him. She gritted her teeth. "Then call the mayor and get me reassigned…again."

"Can't." Disgust weighed heavily in his voice.

"Why not?" Rebecca fought to control the near desperation sliding through her system. This was bad. Real bad.

"Already tried. Mayor wants you here real bad for some reason." His eyes narrowed as he watched her. Suspicion flared in those murky depths.

"That doesn't make sense, why would he care?" She scowled at him.

He shrugged. "Says, it'll be good for the community to have a girl cop runnin' around."

She felt the heat of anger crawl up her neck. "I am not a 'girl cop'. I am a police officer and I take that very seriously, Sheriff Montgomery."

He studied her as he chewed on his pen. "Things are different here in the South, Officer Sugar, especially in the country. Maybe you forgot that, living in the big city for so long. You see, sometimes we have to go more on instinct than by the book. There's a time to be serious, Becca, and there's a time to…relax." He sat up, dropped the pen on the desk and leaned forward, meeting her gaze. "The people of Jericho haven't changed much. They're essentially good, hard-working, people. Farming community, mostly. We have very little call for police enforcement and I already have enough men. I don't need some hard-nosed gal comin' around here hollerin', 'I am woman, hear me roar.'"

Clenching her teeth, Rebecca fought the urge to roll her eyes. "Sheriff, I have no agenda and believe it or not, I'm not a women's libber. I'm a cop. I don't want to be classified by my sex. Just try to ignore the fact that I'm a woman, it has nothing to do with my ability to do my job..."

"But see, Officer Becca Sugar, your sex isn't easily ignored."

She closed her eyes on an exasperated sigh. "Look, let's put everything aside and just call me Officer Taylor."

"Can't."

"Why? Just because you've known me all my life—"

"Because I've tasted your sweet hot pussy, that's why." His expression was sardonic but his voice held a note of anger. "And make no mistake, sweetness, it left me with a terrible craving for more."

She stared at him, momentarily struck dumb with shock. He did not just say that. Oh, but yes he did. He watched her with lowered lids. Her body tensed. He was remembering, and now so was she. She felt the heat curl through her and the corner of his mouth tilted.

"Sheriff Montgomery, what happened last night will never happen again." She gave him a level look.

His laugh was an ominous rumble from deep in his chest. "If you figure no two *good* fucks are ever the same—and we are good at it, Becca—it's only gonna get better." He spoke low and seductive which had her juices flowing.

She clenched her teeth, fighting to control her lust and her temper. She could control this situation and she could handle this hick cowboy, no problem. "How adolescent," she grumbled.

His smile didn't reach his eyes. Arching a brow, he murmured, "Did you expect this country sheriff would be simple? Did you think I'd just hump you and be grateful that you let me have a fancy ride?"

"What?" She felt as if he'd punched her. Her mouth dropped open and she stared at him in disbelief.

"You didn't expect to have the fuck of your life, did ya? You didn't think I could rock your world like those hoity-toity city boys you're used to screwin'. What did you think would happen, Becca, when you decided to fuck the boss?"

Rebecca blinked. She fought for breath. Fought to keep from trying to wipe that superior smug smile off his handsome face.

"For God's sake. I had no idea you were the sheriff last night. I asked to transfer to Jericho because I missed home, I wanted to slow down, get away from the city..." she tried to explain, fighting to draw precious air into her lungs.

"Oh baby, you call that slow? Fast would have killed me! I bet you couldn't wait to show old Jackson the new and improved Pixie Pest."

Okay, this was turning ugly; she could feel it, see it in his glittering silver eyes piercing her. "Look, I didn't mean for that to happen. I just wanted to meet some people, see if anyone I knew was still here, maybe dance, and possibly have a good time and go home...alone. I came to Jericho because I needed a fresh start, in a new place, I wanted to see if this could be home again."

He lifted a brow. "Did you screw up or something in Detroit? What didja do, fuck the chief of police? Or maybe the mayor, ugh...that's not a good mental image, maybe that's why he's all hot and bothered for you to stay."

She glared at him. She was stunned and for some reason, the things he said hurt worse than she thought they should. Fury and humiliation rose like bile in her throat and she stood slowly, keeping her gaze on him. She saw the flash of regret but it did nothing to dissolve the lump in her throat. "Fine, I'll get in touch with the mayor myself and see what I can do. I'm sorry to have wasted your time."

"Damn, okay wait, Becca, just wait." He rubbed his hand over his face and motioned for her to sit again but she stood, her hand resting on the doorknob. "I apologize. I guess that was uncalled for."

She swallowed the knot that was lodged in her throat, lifted a brow and continued to glare at him. "You guess?"

"Talking to the mayor won't do you any good. I fought with him all morning over this. Even before I knew you were female...or that you were...you." He waved a hand at her.

"I don't want anything from you, Jackson. I don't want a relationship, sexual or otherwise. Last night wasn't supposed to happen. I didn't come here to seduce you." She raised her hand when he started to speak and fought to keep from shaking. "And with all due respect, Sheriff, I don't give a good goddamn what you think of me. Just know what happened last night won't happen again, and no matter what you believe, I'm not a nympho on the prowl. So you don't have to worry about the other officers."

He nodded and looked away for the first time, putting his hands on his hips. "It's not about you being a woman, Becca."

"Rebecca," she snapped.

His raised his gaze to hers without raising his head. "It's not about your...sex." She started to retort when something in his narrowing eyes made her hesitate. "Like I said, I don't need you. I didn't expect you. Now that I have you I don't know what to do with you." He combed his fingers though his hair and sighed. Something about the simple frustrated movement brought visions of his naked body rising over her, his sweaty muscles bunching and rippling as he strained toward release.

She swallowed hard. "Like *I* said, I'll talk to the mayor." She turned and fumbled with the doorknob, desperate to get away from him. He walked up behind her and reached around to open the door. She could feel the heat of his body at her back. His scent teased her, making it hard for her to breathe. When did she become so weak, she wondered? Maybe she was a nympho.

"Becca."

She took several steps away from him before she turned around. "Rebecca... What?"

She looked up at him; his eyes had softened, darkened. "It won't do any good..." For a moment, she thought he guessed her reaction and she frowned. "...arguing with the mayor."

"I'll try anyway."

He shrugged. "Matthews!" he shouted down the hall.

"Yeah." The young officer sitting at the desk poked his head around the corner.

"Show Officer B...Taylor around. Make sure she gets a uniform, order one if need be."

Matthews' bright blue eyes assessed Rebecca. "Sure thing, Sheriff." He grinned.

Jackson turned back to Rebecca, his face expressionless. "Officer Bryan Matthews will take care of whatever you need." Then he turned on his heel and sauntered back into his office, slamming the door behind him.

Chapter Seven

The echo of the door slamming grated on Jackson's ears. Anger surged through his body, pounded in his bloodstream, but not for the reason Becca thought. It had nothing to do with sex...at least, not the male/female type. It had everything to do with the fact that his swollen cock pulsed and throbbed in aching demand to bury itself between her thighs. Now. Hard. Feeling the slap of flesh against flesh, hearing her throaty little moans, her cries of completion.

He groaned, kicking his desk, wincing as the toe of his boot met solid oak. Dammit, he didn't need this. Not right now. He sure as hell didn't need Mayor Whittaker thinking he could pull the wool over his eyes this easy. Hell, he had been working for six months now to figure out what the slimy bastard was up to, and he threw one roadblock after another at Jackson.

Somehow, Jackson knew, Whittaker had arranged the former sheriff, Jackson's uncle's, accident, just as Jackson knew that old John Porter had been on to something that the mayor was up to. That was the reason Jackson had fought for the position after John's death. Even going so far as to secure the approval of the Town Council, who in turn pressured Whittaker.

He threw himself into his chair, slouching in it, his lips twisting in a grimace as his eyes narrowed on the door. Damn, he hadn't wanted to leave Becca earlier. His erection had throbbed in protest, his muscles reluctant to lift him from the bed. He should have stayed. At least he could have found the sweet haven of her body once more before it all backfired in his face. Now he was going to have to figure out what the hell was going on here. Whittaker must be running real damned scared if he was letting a woman on the force in the hopes of distracting Jackson. Which to a point, Jackson admitted, was working.

Dammit all to hell. This was a complication he just didn't need. And to make it worse, he had hurt her. He had seen the flash of hurt and disillusionment in her eyes when he had accused her of fucking the mayor. He grimaced, irritated with the surging jealousy that had washed over him while he was on the phone with Whittaker. Damned bastard carrying on about how pretty little Rebecca Taylor had grown up and was all woman now. His snide, insinuating voice as slimy as eel's skin as he touted Rebecca's obvious charms. Furious jealousy had spread through Jackson like a sickness he couldn't combat.

And it wasn't like he hadn't known better. Jackson was well aware of where Rebecca had spent last night. She was in his arms, milking his cock like a fist every time he pushed it in her. Yet Whittaker, for reasons Jackson couldn't explain, had insinuated that she had been otherwise entertained. And not ten minutes after getting off the phone with the bastard, fury still roaring like a live beast through his body, Rebecca had walked in.

His luck sucked. He closed his eyes. He didn't want to think about sucking. But he couldn't help imagining that hot little mouth wrapped around him, her breathy moans vibrating against his cock. He didn't think he could stand it. The whole time she had stood before him, her expression stiff and unyielding, he had wanted to throw her across his desk and rip those damned clothes off her body.

He groaned. He was miserable. He had been looking forward to leaving work later in the day, swinging by her house, seeing if there wasn't more to be found than just the hot sex they'd discovered last night.

His eyes widened. He hadn't used a condom. Son of a bitch. He sat up straight, his hands gripping the armrests of the large padded chair as he swallowed past the sudden lump in his throat. The threat of STD's didn't bother him. He had the printout of her latest blood tests, her overall health check, lying on his desk. She was clean. He was clean. But protection; he had pumped his seed into her body more than once. He breathed out hard. Damn, he hadn't even thought to use a condom.

He ran his hands through his hair, his lips pursing at the thought. She hadn't said anything, but that didn't mean squat. That little spitfire would have kept her mouth shut if it was killing her. Plain fury, unadulterated, had washed through her the whole time she stood in his office. Not that he blamed her. Hell, he hadn't gone easy on her.

"Hey, boss," Bryan Matthews called through the door, knocking sharply at the frosted glass.

"Yeah." Jackson sat back in his chair, wondering at the hesitancy in the kid's voice.

Bryan was twenty-one, fresh out of the academy, and still a little wet behind the ears, but a good kid.

Jackson watched as the younger man shifted nervously, his blue eyes looking at everything but Jackson.

"Umm, no one will ride with her." Bryan closed the door behind him.

It took a minute for Jackson to assure himself that he had heard correctly.

"What?" Jackson asked him, his voice controlled. Dammit.

Bryan's blue eyes met his nervously.

"They won't ride with her, Jackson. Roby and Martin headed out, sayin' no woman was ridin' with them. That just leaves me. I don't care if she rides with me."

Bryan shifted, nervous, on the edge of excitement at the thought. Great. Miss Ree-Becca Taylor had another conquest. Damn, if she wasn't sure picky about that name.

But that didn't alleviate his concern where Roby and Martin were concerned. Their refusal to ride with her smacked of discrimination. If there was one thing the department didn't need, it was a discrimination suit.

"Okay. Let her ride with you, but don't let her take over, Bryan," he warned the boy. "That's one woman, if you give her a chance, that'll run right over you."

Bryan's eyes widened. "Aw, Jack, she's a sweet little thing." He laughed at the thought. "Just because she's a Yankee doesn't mean you have to watch her. Course, watching her will be fun." The male look of approval could get the boy decked, Jackson thought.

"We've had Yankees here before, Bryan. You're starting to sound like your grandfather. They're not a different species from us, you know?" Jackson reminded him. "Besides, Becca was born and raised here. She's not really a Yankee."

"I know. But Officer Taylor is sure an improvement to the force." He smiled, his too innocent blue eyes reflecting his growing awareness of Becca's female qualities.

Jackson frowned.

"Don't start, Bryan. She's a fellow officer. Remember the sexual harassment classes we all had to take?" Pain in the ass. Like they didn't know they weren't supposed to grope an employee's ass.

Jackson frowned. Damned if Officer Becca didn't have an ass well worth groping.

"Yeah, I know." Bryan grinned. "I promise, I won't sexually harass her. But that sure don't mean I can't look. I'll go let her know. Hell, maybe I'll even let her drive my cruiser. That oughta make her feel good."

Jackson lowered his brows as the young officer left the room. Let her drive his cruiser? Bryan was severely underestimating Officer Ree-Becca Taylor. She would most likely insist on it. Determination and stubbornness sat on her shoulders like mantles of pride. Damn, getting back into her pants wasn't going to be easy. It was going to be damned hard if he didn't do something fast. He needed information. One sure way to find your opponent's weakness was to arm yourself with knowledge.

Grinning at that, he picked up the phone and punched in a familiar number. Ted Mason, an officer with the Illinois State Police Force could get the answers he needed. And he owed Jackson. Owed him big.

"Mason." The burly trooper answered on the first ring.

"Hey, Ted, it's Jackson. How's my sister doing?" Jackson didn't even try to smother his laughter.

"Damn you, Jack, that woman's driving me crazy. Do you know she painted the front room purple? Freaking purple. What drives that woman?"

Jackson held the phone away from his mouth. He couldn't control his laughter on that one.

"Laugh it up. You'll be laughing when I cart her ass back to Hicksville to you," Ted threatened good-naturedly. "Now why the hell are you calling? If you wanted to check on Candy, you could have called her yourself."

Jackson sighed.

"I need a check run on one of Chicago's former finest," he told him, liking the way Ted took care of business first. "Name's Rebecca Taylor. Age twenty-six. She just transferred to Jericho, and I need to know why."

There was silence across the line for a long moment.

"Fat ole Tommy Whittaker pulled in a female officer?" Ted asked suspiciously. "The same male chauvinist, no-female-on-my-force, Whittaker?"

"Yep, that's the one." Jackson leaned back in his chair. "I need to know what the hell's up with this. It's fishy."

"Hell yeah." Silence stretched again. When Ted came back he was all business. "You think this has anything to do with Porter's death?"

"I don't, Ted, but something doesn't feel right about it. Whittaker didn't tell me who my new deputy was, or even when she was showing up. I was led to believe it was a male for weeks. I need to know what's up with it."

"You think she's involved?"

Ted was one of the few people aware of Jackson's investigation of the mayor.

Jackson frowned. "I don't think she is. But hell if I know for sure. I knew her way back, Ted, when she was just a little thing. I'd hate to think she was involved with that bastard."

"I'll see what I can find. In the meantime, I heard an interesting rumor the other day that I wanted to run by you. We picked up an illegal a few days ago. Middle Eastern. He's suspected of being part of a terrorist cell operating in these parts. Says he spent a few days in Jericho back in the winter, hiding from the Feds. You have a Middle Eastern population I didn't know about?"

Jackson frowned. Other than ole Doc Mustafa, there was no one.

"Not that I was aware of. Should I be checking for one?"

Ted sighed in disgust. "Naw. Guess not. The information just caught my attention as kind of odd. Just keep your eyes open, let me know if you see anyone odd."

Jackson shook his head. He hadn't seen or heard of Middle Eastern visitors to the area. Jericho was pretty laid back and off the beaten track, and since Nine-Eleven, pretty damned suspicious of everyone.

"I'll see what I can find out," Jackson nodded. "But I haven't heard of anything through rumor. I'll check it out though."

"You do that, and I'll hold Candy off from that visit she wants to make home." Jackson winced. He didn't need Candy here right now.

"You do that thing there, Ted. Promise me for sure." Jackson shook his head. Damn, Candy could throw a monkey wrench in his plan's right fast. The last thing he needed was his baby sister finding out he was working with a woman, much less that he was attracted to her. Attracted…ha, that was a gross understatement.

"Good plan then. I'll get back to you in a day or two," Ted said decisively. "Later there, bro."

Bro. Jackson swallowed his laughter. Ted only called him bro when he was put out with Candy, his little southern honey.

Jackson disconnected, frowning thoughtfully. He could put out a few feelers, check things out. He was pretty certain there was no place in Jericho to hide illegals without someone hearing about it. Newcomers stood out like a sore thumb and Arabics would definitely be noticed. Until then, he had a woman to woo. Damn, if he didn't get back into that woman's bed right soon, he would burst his jeans to hell and back with the hard-on throbbing between his thighs. He shifted in his chair, hoping to ease the pressure. He sighed in bleak acceptance long minutes later. No ease.

Chapter Eight

Jackson made his round of Jericho the next afternoon, watching the traffic and the pedestrians thoughtfully. There was no such thing as coincidence, he thought. The knowledge that Ted's illegal had spent time in Jericho worried at Jackson's mind.

Whittaker was a crooked, dirty son of a bitch, but a smart one. Jackson had been investigating for over a year now, ever since the death of the former sheriff, Jackson's uncle, Tobias Montgomery.

Jackson had returned to Jericho after his release from active duty in the Marines. Tobias had been distracted, worried, rather than jovial and outgoing as he usually was. It had taken Jackson six months to find out that his uncle was investigating the mayor. To that point, the county judge had drowned on a fishing trip, despite the fact that the lake was as calm as a pond and that Judge Morris had not been an old man. He had also been an excellent swimmer.

The sheriff's office was staffed with Whittaker's men, Tobias had informed him, men he had once counted as friends. And the mountains were getting damned dangerous to hike in. The amount of "hunting accidents" that had occurred over the months had whipped Tobias into a rage. Not two months later, Tobias was dead too. Hunting accident, the coroner had said. Jackson wasn't a fool, he knew better.

Jackson frowned as he drove through town. What connection did Whittaker and Ted's suspected terrorist share? There had to be one. His fingers tapped at the steering wheel as his mind blazed with possibilities. Tobias had been certain Whittaker was hiding something. What could he have been hiding? Or could it have been who? The possibilities that came to mind terrified him.

He made a turn on Main Street and headed out of town, knowing that there were few places within the city limits to hide anyway. Too many gossips and nosy shopkeepers to spill the beans. The problem with small towns was that everyone knew your business, and where you took it. Made for interesting dinner conversation, but not secrecy. If someone was out to hide, or hide others, it would have to be farther into the mountains. That was most often considered no man's land, the shadowed, mysterious world of Indian legends, illegal stills, and mountain folk.

Times had changed a lot though, Jackson told himself as he made the journey from the bustle of Jericho along the two lane road that led farther up the mountain. Even since he was a boy, civilization had begun to creep stealthily into the higher parts of the mountains. Electric lines, telephone cable, computers and cell phones were the norm now. Broken down shacks were replaced with modern frame houses, and pickups graced front yards and driveways of even the most uninhabitable reaches.

One such place was Jacob Riley's cabin. It was a bitch and three quarters to get to, and if the cruiser Jackson had earmarked for the department wasn't a four-wheel drive jeep, then he would have been making a hell of a long walk. But Jacob knew things. And what he didn't know, he could damned well find out. If there were terrorists hiding anywhere in those mountains, then he likely knew about it.

The jeep bounced over the long, pitted road up to Jacob's cabin. The vehicle's engine whined as it struggled over large rocks, eroded ditches and broken brush. He had told Jacob more than once that he needed the road graveled, perhaps even blacktopped, but it appeared he was still being ignored.

Finally, he pulled into a well-kept driveway, grated, graveled and leveled, and shook his head in exasperation. The small log cabin sat on a slope above him, the windows dark, the door tightly closed.

Jackson got out of the jeep, moving quickly to the front door, when the first sounds penetrated. The hungry, gasping female moan was almost a shock. Hell, he thought Jacob was a monk of some kind. The sounds of pleasure rose as Jackson turned and walked to the back of the cabin.

He stopped at the side of the house, shaking his head as he pulled his glasses from his eyes and stared in shock at the scene before him. Jacob had a pretty little black-haired business type stretched over the picnic table, her narrow skirt around her waist, her white silk blouse opened. Hell, it looked like he'd cut her bra open rather than unhooking it from the back.

The woman's deep black hair had escaped the knot that struggled to stay secure on the top of her head. Stray wisps clung in damp strands along her cheek and neck. A fine film of perspiration glazed the woman's pale skin and Jacob's broad naked back.

The woman's legs were splayed wide, giving Jackson an unimpeded view of the soft flesh the mountain man was plowing vigorously into. The soft sounds of wet cunt and hard cock filled the air. Slapping flesh overlaid it, and adding to the arousing mix was the woman's ever-increasing moans as Jacob drove her closer to climax.

Her hands were gripping Jacob's arms, nails pressing into flesh. Her body arched, her full breasts, tipped with hard nipples and flushed with lust, were a damned tempting sight. Almost as pretty as Becca's berry tipped breasts.

He felt a shade of discomfort at his voyeurism. But damn, it was just one of those sights you couldn't look away from. He couldn't believe that Jacob had allowed himself a second moment of vulnerability. The first had been near fatal. Jackson assured himself that he just wanted to be certain Jacob stayed safe while immersed in his pleasure.

As Jackson watched, Jacob's thrusts increased. The sound of balls slapping against a rounded ass filled the air. The woman jerked, arched, her head was thrown back as she began to beg in desperation for release. Then she was crying out, her body stiffening as Jacob drove into her hard, deep. The sounds of their mingled climaxes had Jackson shifting uncomfortably. Damn if he hadn't wished he had gone back to the jeep instead. The woman's cries were much too reminiscent of Becca, reminding him how tight and hot her cunt was around his flesh. He sure hoped she got over her mad soon.

"Dammit, Jack, this ain't no peep show." Jacob was breathing hard as he moved away from the woman, jerking her skirt over her exposed flesh, then fastening his jeans quickly. "What the hell are you doing here?"

He helped the woman from the table, shielding her face with his big body as she fought to fix her clothes. He whispered something to her; Jackson couldn't make out the words. But there was a surprising edge of tenderness as Jacob touched her cheek, kissed her brow quickly.

"Taking notes." Jackson grinned. "That's some fine form you got going there, my friend. I say you should give lessons."

The brawny ex-cop frowned back at him, his brown eyes narrowing dangerously as he stood in front of the woman. Then he turned back to her, tucked a strand of hair back from her face and sighed heavily.

"Go on inside." He nodded at the open back door. "I'll be there as soon as I shove this bastard off my mountain."

The woman flushed, tugging her blouse closed and rushing away from Jackson's curious gaze.

"You used to have better manners," Jacob grunted angrily as he sprawled out in one of the large, wooden chairs beneath the shade of a nearby tree. "What the hell happened?"

Jackson flushed, but fought to ignore it.

"And you used to hear better." Jackson shrugged. "Must have been a while for you if you didn't hear me cursing you as I came up this mountain."

"I heard your jeep. You need a tune up," Jacob snarled. "Now what the hell are you doing here?"

Jackson walked over to a matching chair and sat down heavily. He needed Jacob's help; he couldn't afford to alienate him right now.

"I heard a report there's illegals hiding somewhere in my county. I thought I'd head up here and see if you've noticed anything." If anyone knew, it would be Jacob.

Jacob grunted sarcastically. "Lot of things go on in these mountains."

That was the damned truth. It was becoming dangerous to even attempt hunting anymore.

"Yep, and you seem to know who's doing the better part of it and where they can be found," Jackson said, watching his friend thoughtfully.

Jacob shrugged.

"Heard you have a new officer." The other man grinned tightly, his brown eyes sharp.

Jackson sighed and relaxed back in his chair. He didn't know what the hell kind of game Jacob was playing, but evidently he knew something after all.

"Yeah. I do."

"I hear that pretty little thing left the Wild Rose with a redneck sheriff her first night in, and he followed her right fast to her new house and spent the night. You shootin' for trouble with Mayor 'Fancypants' or just stumbling into it?"

Jackson felt a strange sense of unease at Jacob's words.

"If there's trouble, then I guess I've stumbled into it," he said with a smile. "But damn, Jacob, that little lady would be more than worth it."

Jacob sighed wearily, glancing at the house.

"Yeah, some of 'em are worth it." He swiped his fingers through his overly long blond hair, then ran his hand over his scarred chest.

The burns had healed, but the scars were still there. A reminder of the fiery crash that had nearly taken his life. The tall blond hulk had been one of the best-damned detectives in Nashville until he came upon a few dirty cops, and a drug deal. One of the cops had been his fiancée, the other her lover.

"Now what the hell's going on?" Jackson leaned forward, watching his friend expectantly. "And don't bother to tell me you don't know anything."

Jacob shook his head. "I don't have anything concrete yet," he told him. "But that sweet thing plying her wares in the house seems to be after the same thing, but different agenda. I think she's a journalist, but I can't be sure. She swears she's a lawyer. And there's some damned strange movement around the camping area outside of Jericho, up around Sid Carter's place. I just haven't been able to get away from Sweet Thing long enough to check it out."

The camping area in question was a government deal, but privately run. It was set back from the main road, the camping spots situated for privacy. Through the summer, RV's of every shape and size made use of it.

"In the camping area?" Jackson asked him quietly.

"No." Jacob shook his head. "Back along the mountain there are some damned hideaways easily accessible to a SUV or four-wheel drive. The caves run for miles, and it would make a hell of a hiding place. But you'd have to know where to go looking."

Jackson grimaced.

"Have you seen anyone out that way?"

Jacob scratched his cheek thoughtfully. "Seen some strangers, a few Middle Eastern types about a month back, then they just disappeared. A week later Miss Hot Pants shows up and we've been going around and around ever since. So far, I don't know shit. I just suspect." Which was damned near the same thing.

"And you didn't get hold of me for what reason?" Jackson arched a brow with mocking patience. Son of a bitch was getting too damned reclusive.

"Because I wasn't sure," Jacob explained mockingly.

"That wouldn't have stopped you before, Jake," he bit out. "What the hell's going on in these mountains, anyway? You used to call me weekly."

"Yeah, I did." Jacob nodded, watching him carefully. "Then last time I called you sent that fuck-up Martin out to take a statement. Figured you'd done had enough of me."

Jackson didn't bother to hide his surprise.

"This would have been when?" he snapped. "I've never sent Martin out here, Jake."

Jake grimaced. "I wondered about that. Fact is, I left a message while you were out one day that I needed to talk to you about a patch I had found. Next thing I know, Martin is on my doorstep threatenin' to arrest me for growing it. I played real casual, waited a day or two and went to check it out again. It was gone."

Jackson was silent. He had received no messages that Jacob had called, no memo, no nothing.

"Who took the message?" he asked, his voice soft.

Jacob shrugged. "I'm not sure who took it. Said it was Bryan, but didn't sound much like Bryan. Too old, I thought. But who the hell knows?"

Jackson knew it wasn't Bryan. If there was one person on the force he knew wouldn't lie to him, then it was Bryan.

"I have a report that a terrorist was picked up not too long ago, and claimed to have spent some time around here hiding. If we have terrorists using our mountains, Jacob, then no one is safe, anywhere."

Jacob tapped the fingers of his left hand on the armrest of his seat. He gazed out across the valley, his eyes narrowed, his expression hard.

"You think Whittaker has a game going with those bastards?" he asked Jackson, his voice hard and cold.

"I think it's possible," Jackson sighed. "Think you could check the area for me anytime soon?" Jackson glanced toward the house, wondering where Jake's bit of fluff had gone off to. "If I start nosing around, it could scare them off. I want to know what the hell's going on and who's behind it."

Jacob grinned. "Yeah, I'll ditch her soon enough. I was just waiting on you to get curious and head up here. Give me a week or two and I'll see what I can find out for you."

"Call me on the cell phone, don't bother with the office," Jackson told him, standing to his feet, tension radiating along his body. He was being fucked in his own office and it wasn't sitting well with him. But it was no more than he had expected since taking the job after his uncle's death. He could only imagine how Tobias had felt.

"Will do." Jacob nodded. "You watch your back though, buddy. Martin is the mayor's little ass kisser, and if he's dirty dealing then you can bet that old bastard is behind it."

Jackson grunted. He knew that well.

"I'm heading back down then." He tucked his glasses back on his face, trying to stem the anger flowing through his body.

"I'll be in touch," Jacob nodded.

Jackson left the yard and strode quickly back to the jeep. Son of a bitch, just what he needed right now, a fucking conspiracy.

CHAPTER NINE

Rebecca stomped into the building, her hands fisted at her sides. Her hair was pulled from her bun and she was sure a bruise was blooming along her left cheekbone. Adrenalin drove her, she'd had enough of this petty "boys' club" shit and now she was out for blood. Bryan came out of the restroom and almost collided with her on her way to the break room.

He jumped back, his eyes wide as he took in her appearance and expression. "Damn, Rebecca, what happened?"

"Domestic disturbance. Route 109. The Millers." She just wanted a cold pop and some ice for her throbbing cheek.

"You shoulda called for back up. Those two are vicious."

Rebecca gave Bryan a look that had him lifting his hands and taking a step back.

Officers Ed Martin and Roby Davis came through the front door; their noisy jibes and chuckles were like spikes through her skull. She spun around and marched back to where they stood. They turned on her, Ed with his mocking grin. Roby just leered.

"Where the hell were you two?" Her jaw was clenched.

"We was patrolin', Officer Taylor. What were you doin'?" Ed asked, his hands on his fat hips.

"Cut the shit! I called for back up," she growled through her teeth, shaking with fury. Fantasies of plowing her fists into their fat faces played in her mind, tempting her. Her short nails bit into her palms as she fought to keep them at her sides.

"Well yeah, but we was otherwise occupied and couldn't get to you." They looked at one another. Ed winked. "'Sides,

Taylor, you're from the big city, the streets of Detroit. You tellin' us you couldn't handle a bickerin' couple?"

She stared at them both incredulously. Dear God, no one was safe with these two idiots on patrol. "Oh, I handled them, Officers," she said in a snide tone. "They're both disarmed and locked up tight in the patrol car for now. Mr. Miller needs stitches." Frustration and rage were churning in her stomach. Her cheek stung and her attitude was just getting worse, and if she didn't get some distance between them she was going to hurt someone. "To hell with it, I need a pop." She turned to walk away.

"A pop?" Roby asked. "Looks like you done had you a pop, missy."

That was it, the last straw. The tight grip Rebecca had on her restraint slipped. She whirled around and charged, only to be caught around the waist. She struggled in vain against the steely arm that held her and kicked back, hoping to connect with a shin. Jackson set Rebecca down, meeting her sharp gaze with one of his own, when she twisted around, fists raised. She rolled her shoulder, breathing heavily through her nose, but dropped her hands. Nevertheless, Jackson laid his hand tightly on her shoulder. He stared at Roby then looked at each of them in turn, his eyes narrowing at Rebecca, then he looked at Bryan. "What in the hell is going on?" Roby started to answer but quickly shut his mouth with a piercing glare from Jackson.

Ever the peacemaker, Bryan stepped in. "Sheriff, from what I can gather, Officer Taylor answered a call on a domestic disturbance, the Millers again. Anyway, she called for back up and it seems Officers Martin and Davis were otherwise occupied and failed to assist. However, Officer Taylor neutralized the situation and has the Millers in custody. Mr. Miller needs stitches."

Jackson turned his head and looked at Rebecca. She met his gaze with defiance. His lips were pressed together, the muscle in his jaw pulsed. She assumed his teeth were clenched. He released her shoulder. Her eyes widened as his hand cupped her face and she winced as he ran his thumb over the bruise. The electric current that ran through her at his touch contrasted with the anger she felt that he would touch her like that in front of fellow officers. She pulled away and he let his hand drop.

"I'll expect your full report, Officer Taylor, today." He turned to the officers who stood scowling at Rebecca. "You left a fellow officer in danger? You'd better have a damn good reason for it. Matthews, help Martin and Davis get Mrs. Miller into the holding cell." Then turning to the two officers, "After you've taken Mr. Miller for his stitches and get him squared away, I want to see you both in my office. Clear?"

"Crystal," Roby muttered.

"My office. Now, Rebecca!" He turned and walked away.

Rebecca watched him walk to his office. He left the door open, expecting her to obey. Considering the fact that he was her boss, he should expect no less. But she'd be damned if she'd let him treat her like a Pixie Pest. She walked slowly to the office. He stood beside his desk, hands on his hips, grim expression on his face.

"Close the door."

"I don't think—"

"Rebecca! Close the fuckin' door." She clenched her teeth, reached behind her and slammed the door shut. He walked around the desk and sat in his chair. Leaning forward, he rested clasped hands on the desk. "Sit," he commanded.

Like hell, she thought. "I'm fine standing."

"Officer Taylor, sit down and stop defying me."

She sneered at him and sat.

"Tell me what happened." He watched her, his eyes intent on her every move. It unnerved her, made her feel hot and irritated.

"Bryan already told you everything."

"Details."

With a sigh she told him about the neighbor calling it in. "I responded and found Mrs. Miller wielding a knife, Mr. Miller with a shotgun ranting and raving."

"I can get that from the report," he snapped. "Tell me about Martin and Davis. You called for back up?"

"Yes."

"And the response was?"

"They said, 'In a minute, we're busy with something.'"

His expression was incredulous. "That's their exact words."

"Yes. Look, Sheriff, I'm not trying to be a bitch here but I need to be able to trust my fellow officers when I go into a hostile situation. I'm brave and I'm tough but I'm not stupidly so. I'm not going to risk my life for nothing."

Jackson arched a brow and stood. "I agree." He walked around to stand in front of her. Leaning back against the desk he reached out and touched her cheek. "Were you hurt anywhere else?"

"I'm fine."

"Stand up."

"Sheriff, I'm fine," she said, meeting his hard gaze.

"I said, stand up. God, you're still as stubborn as always." He frowned at her.

She stood stiffly. He cupped her face in his hands, gently probing for further injury. She held still, hoping he could see the warning in her eyes. "It's only a bruise," she said in disgust, trying to pull away.

"How did you get it?"

"Mr. Miller backhanded me. But I put him down. No big deal."

"Is this your only injury?" His voice was strained and violent.

"Yes. Now will you stop touching me?" she questioned with frustration.

"No," he murmured and moved closer and kissed the bruise.

"Don't, Jackson. This is a bad idea," she whispered and put her hands on his shoulders.

She nearly moaned as the bulge of his arousal rubbed against her lower stomach. "It's a good idea, Becca." He spoke softly against her lips. She could taste coffee and him. The slight touch sent spirals of lust through her. "Really, really good."

His mouth moved over hers with a hunger that pulled at her. Her heart pounded. Her brain screamed at her to pull away as her arms went around him, her fingers digging into his muscled back. His hands speared through her hair holding her there as his tongue mated with hers. She couldn't help thinking of that talented tongue traveling her body. Her nipples contracted painfully, wanting his attention. Almost as if he read her mind and body, his hand moved to the buttons of the polyester uniform shirt. She hated the damn uniform and its ugly material, uncomfortable as hell, and right now…it was separating her skin from his. She nearly melted when he nibbled her neck and spoke quietly against her skin.

"I love it when you turn pink for me. Your skin is so hot against my tongue." He licked her collarbone. "Mmm, baby you taste so good."

He finally had her shirt unbuttoned, and he bent and kissed the swells above the top of her lacy bra. With one hand he unsnapped the front clasp of her bra, freed her breasts, and licked the mark he'd left on her. Her nipples pressed against his palms. His hands traveled down her body and circled her waist, then he lifted her and sat her on his desk as he moved between her thighs.

"Ohmigod, Jackson, stop, we have to stop," she whimpered.

"No we don't," was his muffled reply. "God, Becca, I've been starving for you."

His mouth closed over one nipple and she nearly cried out. She ran her hand through his wild hair, holding him closer to her. Her other hand slid down his tight stomach to the raging erection pressing urgently against the front of his pants. She unzipped them and closed her hand over his shaft. It was thick and hard as stone, hot and pulsing in her hand. He groaned against her breast. Her thumb smoothed over the swollen velvety head of his cock and she felt the slick dew that welled at the tip. It thrilled her, this effect she had on him. The way he became wild with want of her.

His hand was cupping her now; she ground her mound against his hand. She was so close to shattering, and so was he. She could feel his body quaking as she slid her hand firmly up and down along his rigid shaft. It was so hard, so thick. She bit her lip and wondered if she dared slide him inside her clenching vagina. She wanted him pumping hard inside her body. He continued to rub her and suck at her nipples. Her head fell back as she undulated against him.

"Jackson..." She was just about to ask him to fuck her hard when there was a knock at the door. They grabbed each other, panting for breath. Jackson let her go, his hot gaze reflecting the unfulfilled lust in her own. The air was thick with tension, frustration. It had Jackson baring his teeth as he quickly zipped his pants. She should be ashamed, she thought breathing deeply as she jumped down from the desk. Jackson went to the door as she turned away to fasten her bra and button her shirt. "Yeah?"

"Uh, Sheriff, there's a call for you. I wouldn't bother you but it's the mayor, sir," Bryan spoke quietly.

"Shit," he whispered harshly. "Okay, put it through."

She walked past him, too fast for him to stop her. "You'll have my report before the end of the day." She met his hot gaze and swallowed then turned and left the office.

Bryan turned and walked backwards. "Hey, you okay?" he asked Rebecca, his brows furrowed over his curious baby blues.

"Yes, why wouldn't I be?" she asked, trying to hide her embarrassment. Did he know what they were doing, what they almost did? He had to guess.

"Well, you look a little flushed. I guess he really gave it to ya, huh?"

"What? What do you mean?" Rebecca felt sick.

Bryan rolled his eyes. "The sheriff, did he ream you out?" Her eyes widened and Bryan looked exasperated. "For going in and dealing with the Millers without waiting for back up."

Rebecca smiled with relief. "Not too bad. Turn around before you run into something." She said as she turned into the restroom and locked the door behind her.

She went to the sink and washed her hands then looked up at her reflection in the mirror. "Oh my God." Either Bryan was terribly naïve or he was pretending to be for her sake. She looked like a wanton woman, a beat up one. Her hair was already loose from the bun so that wasn't too obvious. The bruise on her cheek had puffed up a bit more and now had a purple tinge to it. Her lips were swollen and pink from Jackson's kisses. Her shirt was buttoned wrong. Her neck was pink...he was right. She lifted a hand to her neck with a sigh. She was in trouble. The man had her entranced. His slightest touch had her wanting to strip all her clothes off and pounce on him. She just couldn't get enough.

But, this had to stop. This was her life, her career at stake and when all was said and done and he was finished with her...she paused, looking into her own eyes and pushed aside the dread she saw there...it would be she that suffered. She would lose her job, not the good old boy with the easy grin. No, it would be the stuffy Yank that came back to town to stir up trouble that would get the reprimand and the ax. On top of that, this was just unethical. It was a conflict of interest. It was wrong and she would put a stop to it.

She adjusted her breasts, noting the bluish love bite; she ran her fingers over it lightly and shivered. She sighed and buttoned her shirt correctly then brushed her hair out and piled it back on top of her head. She checked her reflection one last time. "This day can not be over fast enough for me."

* * * * *

"So, ya wanna join us?" Bryan walked beside Rebecca up to the station. He and some of his friends were planning on going to the Wild Rose to hang out, maybe dance a little. All she had on her mind was getting the report to Jackson, getting out of there and heading home to a hot bath and cool sheets.

"I think not tonight. It's only Wednesday. I still have unpacking to do and besides that, I'm exhausted. It's been a day from hell."

"Yeah, well, maybe some other time then."

"Some other time." She gave him a smile when he held the door open. "I really appreciate the invitation, Bryan."

She looked up into Jackson's frowning face. "Do you have that report?"

"Yes." She opened the leather portfolio she was carrying, found the report, handed it to him and started to walk away.

"Wait," he said abruptly without looking up. "I need to see you in my office."

"Sheriff Montgomery, could it wait until tomorrow? It's been a long day and I need to get home and —"

"No, it can't wait."

"Fine." She marched down the hall, her boots noisy on the ugly tile floor. He followed behind.

She stood behind the chair this time. He shut the door quietly and moved up behind her. She whirled around and held up one finger. "Stop!"

He leaned over and sucked her finger in his mouth, nipping at the end. "Don't you think we're past this playing hard to get thing? Or do you have a date with Danger Boy out there?" He sneered at her and by God, it pissed her off. What the hell was his problem? She shoved at his chest and he backed up, only to lean against the desk, crossing his arms over that wide chest.

"I don't have a date with anyone. Bryan is a nice guy, but he's five years my junior. I have enough problems with older men acting like children, dating someone younger is the last thing I need in my life right now." His brow raised slowly, his expression darkening, but she stopped him before he could speak. "This, this, thing between us is over. I will not risk my career this way. And on top of that, it complicates things, adds stress to an already stressful job. If and when people discover what's happening, I will be dragged through the mud."

"Becca, you've had a rough day—"

"Rebecca, and do not patronize me, Jackson, do not underestimate me. I'm not that lovesick Pixie Pest anymore and you need to get that through your head. This needs to stop. I mean it." She was right, she knew she was right even though she could still feel desire coursing through her. Her voice sounded far away to her; deep, hoarse, shaky with residual passion. Her heart pounded in her ears but she knew she had to use logic, not emotion, not passion.

"You don't trust me."

"Hell no, I don't trust you! Jackson, I don't really even know you. You sure as hell don't know me."

A slow smile curled his lips and he nodded. "You're right. We'll fix that, but you don't get to call all the shots, babe."

She tilted her head to the side as her mouth parted in surprise. He hadn't listened to a word she'd said. Lifting her brows she nodded. "Yes, yes I do, Jackson. I said no, and no means no."

"I've never forced you, Becca, I don't intend to start now." He pushed away from the desk and walked toward her. He touched his finger to her chin and tilted her head up to meet his gaze. "But you do what you feel you need to do, and I'll do what I need to do." He leaned down and kissed her gently on the lips then walked out of his office, leaving her standing there in stunned silence.

Chapter Ten

Hours later, Jackson read the reports that came in on the incident. Rebecca's was detailed, thorough and concise. She had been left to handle the Millers alone, at no small threat to herself, due to Roby and Martin's prejudice of her position on the force. Jackson had little doubt the fact that she was a woman was a major consideration. But he sensed there was much more to their refusal to provide backup. Where the hell had they been and what were they up to? Those good ole boys were becoming more trouble than they were worth. And no one went out to the Miller's alone. Yet Rebecca hadn't been warned of this.

For the most part, the squabbling pair did little to cause serious trouble. But each deputy on the force was well aware of the violent tendencies the pair could display when the sheriff's office was called out. No one went in there without backup, for a reason.

Jackson sat at his office desk, staring silently at other reports that lay on the desk before him. There was an air of sarcasm and mockery in each report, nothing overt, but enough to set his hackles up. Roby and Martin were becoming increasingly insubordinate, and Jackson knew he was going to have to confront the mayor over them soon. The only problem was Mayor Whittaker had hired both jackasses over the previous sheriff's head. They were decent deputies and for the most part did their jobs well, until lately. The past year or so the two had caused more problems they had solved. The disturbing information Jacob had given him about Martin only made him more nervous. He narrowed his eyes at the papers, his lips thinning with anger.

There was more going on here, Jackson knew, something that raised the hair on the back of his neck and made suspicion brew within his mind. He didn't like the answers he was coming up with. Tobias had been killed by someone he knew. No way in hell would anyone else have been able to get close enough to make the shooting appear to be a hunting accident.

He narrowed his eyes as he stared down at the files. He had grown up with the two men. He knew their families, and he knew their personalities. Braggarts for the most part, but he hadn't seen any real aggression in either man until lately. Come to think of it, Roby's wife was driving that new car, and his daughter was taking those expensive dance lessons. How was Roby supporting this?

It all came back to the same puzzle that involved Tobias Montgomery's death. They were linked, he knew in his gut they were, but he would be damned if he could figure out where or how.

Shaking his head, Jackson rose to his feet, filed their reports—Rebecca's, then his own—and prepared to leave the office. He wanted to stop by the Wild Rose for a drink before heading home to his solitary bed. Damn Becca and her stubborn hide. After a taste of her, he was addicted. He should be rushing to her place, or she to his, and getting in a few good hours of lovin'. Hell yeah, he could handle that. Instead, he was heading to a damned bar, frustrated as hell.

The Wild Rose was busy. The usual assortment of vehicles lined the graveled parking lot. Customers loitered outside, calling back and forth, laughing uproariously. Seeing the sheriff, they stilled a little. A few smiled and shouted out, "Hey, Sheriff." Even without the uniform, Jackson knew he presented an imposing figure and had earned respect. Sometimes, a fair but hard-nosed attitude kept order a hell of a lot easier than a big stick.

He entered the loud atmosphere of the building. The bar packed to capacity, and more than a little rowdy. Thankfully, the owner kept a few cousins around just in case things got out of hand.

"Hey, Tank," Jackson greeted one of the largest. Seven feet of rough, dumb muscle.

Tank's wide face split into a grin, his nut-brown skin stretching across his homely face as Jackson walked by.

"Hey, Jackson. You see that pretty deputy of yours tonight? Whooey, she's a damned pretty sight."

Jackson stopped, turning back to the bouncer with a questioning look.

"Becca's here?" he asked. Damn her, she was supposed to be at home resting.

"Nursing her drink in the far corner," Tank informed him, beefy hands gesturing to the back of the bar. "That woman done tangled with a wildcat, but she's still pretty as hell."

Jackson shook his head at the woman's stubbornness.

"Thanks, Tank, I'll go see if I can haul her home."

"You do that, Jackson. She don't look up to a crowd, if you ask me." Tank could be dumb, real dumb. But he had smarts where it counted.

Jackson moved quickly through the bar, heading for the far corner, knowing the only private place to be found in the Wild Rose. The dimly lit booth in the back was often used for heated embraces and public copulations rather than one lone sheriff's deputy nursing a hell of a headache and a possible concussion. The blaring music from the jukebox wasn't as sharp there, and the waitress paid little attention to the occupants so Jackson was more than surprised to see one of them setting a fresh drink on the table and moving away quickly. He caught her as she passed him and ordered a drink himself before moving toward the booth once again.

And there Becca sat, that wild hair falling below her shoulders, her face bruised and pale.

"What the hell are you doing here?" He slid into the seat across from her, watching as she raised her head slowly, her eyes narrowing as she stared at him.

"Avoiding you," she sighed in defeat.

Jackson leaned back against the seat, fighting his grin.

"So why not avoid me in the comfort of your home?" he asked her, bracing his elbows on the table as he leaned closer. "Makes more sense than sitting here in the dark with a headache."

"I don't have a headache," she lied. He could see the stress marking her face. He knew she had a headache.

"What did the doctor say?" He had nearly called the doctor himself to get the report.

She mumbled something, and he was certain he misunderstood what she said.

"Repeat that, carefully," he bit out. "I didn't hear you right."

"You heard me just fine," she bit out. "I didn't go to the doctor. I've been hit on the head before. I know what a concussion feels like. I don't have one."

Jackson frowned.

"You have a headache and you're pale—"

"I'm just bruised and I'm pissed off," she bit out, lifting the glass to her lips.

Jackson watched as she sipped heavily at the drink.

"Are you driving tonight?" he asked her cautiously.

Rebecca sighed. "No, I'm not driving. I came in with Bryan. He's around somewhere."

She waved her hand absently after delivering that shocking statement. Jackson didn't like the tight bite of jealousy that attacked his mind like a ravenous wolf. Damn kid. He just didn't know when to leave well enough alone.

"Well, you're leaving with me," he announced firmly, hoping he wasn't leaving any room for argument. Damn woman was too stubborn. "Come on, let's go."

He stood to his feet, staring down at her as he held his hand out to her.

"Why are we leaving?" she asked him suspiciously. "I told you, Jackson, I'm not having sex with you anymore."

"You didn't like my sex, Becca?" he asked her, grinning slow and easy. He knew damned well she liked it. She screamed when she climaxed, that was a hell of an indication.

Her eyes narrowed, glittering dangerously.

Jackson sighed roughly.

"Fine, no sex. But you feel like hell, hon. I can see it. I'll just take you home and tuck you in nice and safe where you can rest." He wondered if he should be crossing his fingers over that lie. It was a whopper. If there was a chance of getting into Ree-Becca's pants tonight, then he wasn't about to let it go by.

The thought of all that smooth, satiny skin, the tight hot grip of her cunt clenching around his cock like a velvet fist, had him hardening immediately. Uh oh. He watched as Becca glanced at the growing bulge in his jeans.

"Ignore him." He shrugged. "He has a mind of his own. He knows who the boss is, though."

Yeah, the boss was that tight little vagina that could clench and milk and make him beg for mercy. Jackson suppressed his groan. Damn, it was going to be a long night if she didn't make her mind up here soon.

"Fine." Rebecca lifted her purse from beside her, slapped some money on the table and rose to her feet. "I need to let Bryan know I'm leaving, though."

Jackson looked around the bar. There was Bryan, his smile turned on a pretty little blonde who gazed up at him with just enough hard edge to have him feeling sorry for the kid. Jackson caught the deputy's eye, and gestured to Rebecca. Bryan nodded.

"Taken care of." Jackson gripped her elbow as she came to her feet. "Come on, Cinderella, let's take you home before you fall on your glass slippers."

"Smartass," she muttered.

Jackson grinned. He moved her quickly through the bar, then into the sultry, humid air of a Tennessee summer night. Becca moved slowly beside him, letting him lead for a change as they walked to his truck. He unlocked her door, helping her in, then locked her in securely before moving to his own side.

The night was quiet, dark. The drive to her house wasn't a long one, giving Jackson little time to try to decide the best way to get her to invite him into the house. Damn, he was dying to taste Becca's heat again.

"You aren't coming in," she announced as they pulled up in front of her house.

Jackson winced.

"I'll see you to the door at least, Becca."

"Do you have a thing against my name?" She flashed him an angry look. "How many times do I have to keep telling you, it's Ree-becca?"

Jackson sighed. Damn, that headache must be a bad one.

"You are a chauvinist," she suddenly announced, her brows lifting over glassy green eyes. "That's why you refuse to use my name."

"No, ma'am." He smiled at her temperamental expression. "I'm no chauvinist. "

"Then why?" she questioned him roughly. "Give me one good reason why you can't call me by my name."

"Takes too long." He shrugged, anticipating the fireworks.

"Excuse me?" Astonishment covered her expression.

"Well." He turned so he faced her, one arm over the steering wheel, the other laying along the back of the seat as he watched her. "It's like this, sugar, I get kinda short on breath just remembering how hot and tight that sweet little pussy of yours was. I can't get all those syllables in your name out of my mouth. So we're stuck with Becca."

Her mouth dropped open and she blinked in angry amazement.

"That's ridiculous," she muttered crossing her arms over her breasts.

"Naw, that's just horny," he sighed. "Real bad horny, sugar. I can't forget how good it was. Have you forgotten?"

Oh no, she hadn't forgotten. It was there in the sudden flush of her cheeks, the over-bright awareness in her eyes. She remembered, and she wanted more. He knew she did. Because he was burning alive for it, and refused to consider he was in it alone.

"Sure you don't want to invite me in?" His hand moved until his fingers were touching the softness of her hair. "I have a great cure for a headache."

He watched her, mentally begging the good Lord above that she would give in and say yes. At the rate he was going, he was going to expire from lust. Hell of a way for a man with a hard dick to have to go. And the part that really irked him, mindless, stubborn bastard that his cock was, that it refused to consider any other warm wet haven than that of Becca's. He was addicted. He sighed, forlorn.

"You're moving too fast for me, Jackson," she whispered, shaking her head, suddenly serious. "I thought I remembered things moving slow and easy in the South? I need some space."

Jackson shrugged. Hell. A woman that had to think about it first.

"That's fine too, sugar," he said easily, though he wanted to grit his teeth. "Come on, let me walk you to your door and do the gentleman thing here so we can both get some sleep. It's been a hell of a day for you."

He got out of the car and moved quickly to the passenger side. Opening the door there, he reached in to grip her arm lightly and help her out. She was warm, and soft. He suppressed his groan. Dammit, he wasn't going to beg.

Her porch light was on, as was a light in her little kitchen. The house looked homey, safe.

"Got your key?" They paused by the door.

Rebecca nodded as she pulled her key chain out of her purse and fitted the key into the lock. Opening the door, she paused on the threshold.

"Thanks for bringing me home, Jackson," she said softly. Her cultured voice, soft and sweet, washed over his aroused body.

"Yeah well, I might have had a reason other than just your comfort in mind." He grinned down at her, watching the answering amusement that came to her eyes. "Go on to bed, sugar. You're worn out."

He bent to give her a soft, gentle kiss goodnight. His lips lingered, though, sipping at the soft curves of her lips as his body heated. Damn, she tasted fine, he thought. Soft and silky and damned hot. His hand cupped the side of her head, his tongue tracing her lips, staying light, gentle. She was tired and sore, and he knew she felt she needed space. He could give her space. Sure he could.

His tongue slid slowly past her lips, dipping into her mouth as she whispered a sigh of longing against him. Her hands were at his chest, her fingers splayed flat over the white cotton of his shirt as her head tilted for him, her lips opening as her tongue touched his. She tasted as sweet as candy. As hot as fire, and he knew he could never get enough.

Jackson forced his body back from her, groaning in torment. Damn, he was sinking fast.

"Get your ass in that house before I fuck you on the porch," he sighed, shaking his head. "If you need me tonight, call."

"Thank you, Jackson." There was a world of weariness in her tone.

"You're welcome, Becca."

"Ree-becca," she reminded him with a frown.

"Whatever." He shrugged, grinning when irritation flashed over her expression. "Go, woman, so I can head home. My cold shower awaits me."

Rolling her eyes, she went into the house, closing the door firmly then turning the lock. Jackson breathed out roughly.

"Damn woman," he muttered, turning and walking back to his truck. Some nights just had to be harder than others.

Chapter Eleven

The morning was proving to be a good one, made even better by the fact that she had the whole day free. She especially liked having at least one day off in the middle of the week. Fewer people meant she could get her shopping done faster and possibly get some things done at home.

The day was going to be another scorcher. It felt so much better to be out of that hot, navy polyester uniform and in her cool shorts and a tank top. Her headache was gone but she was still a bit tired. Jackson's kiss had made it hard to fall asleep. That damned talented mouth of his…she shivered at the memories that flitted through her brain.

Rebecca shook her head. No, she had too much to do to get caught up in erotic daydreams. She yanked on the cart with one final energetic jerk, freeing it from the others. Groceries, she needed to focus on groceries. Her cabinets were bare and so was her fridge. A salad sounded good for lunch, simple and quick and no cooking…no cooking was always good. She might have salad for dinner too. She smiled to herself. Man, the Piggly Wiggly was sadly lacking when it came to fresh produce, but she managed to find what she needed and moved on. If she got all the errands and stuff done, tonight she'd be able to relax and she really, really needed to relax. A hot bubble bath and a good book would be heaven.

Her first week had not turned out as she imagined it would. Her little indiscretions with Jackson had really screwed things up. The tension at work with Jackson's not so subtle innuendos and double-entendres was enough to drive her mad. He'd get close enough that she'd felt his breath on her neck and the heat radiate from that hard, imposing body of his. Every brush of his hand, every stolen kiss, was making it harder and harder for her to remain impassive, to keep her wits about her. And as if that wasn't enough, her fellow officers had been acting like spoiled little teenage boys.

Oh, Bryan was okay. Such a nice guy, he was ever the peacemaker. If it hadn't been for him, the past week would have been hell. Officers Ed Martin and Roby Davis, however, were another story. They only acknowledged her existence when they had no other recourse. This latest fiasco was proof of that. What a pair those two were, damn obnoxious assholes. She smiled, indulging briefly in a violent fantasy that had her standing over the repentant and respectful cops after she'd beaten the crap out of them.

CRASH

"Oh. Sorry…" Rebecca looked up and groaned inwardly.

"Well, hey there, Becca. Ya know, hon…" He leaned over a bit, pretending to whisper. "You shouldn't fantasize about me while operating any kind of vehicle." He frowned and shook his head. "Dangerous, way too dangerous. "

"Ha, ha, ha." She made a face. "Get out of my way."

Jackson moved his cart to the side without unblocking her way and stepped up next to her, scanning the contents of her cart. Her stomach did little flips. Why did he have to smell so good?

"Now, Becca, there's no call to be rude, even if you did become a Yankee city girl." Like a wolf stalking his prey, Jackson's gaze traveled the length of her body. His voice rumbled low and seductive. "Mmmm, sugar, you have got the best set of legs."

Damn, damn, damn. She didn't need this. Why was he here, now, at the Piggly Wiggly of all places? She didn't remember that behemoth he called a truck in the parking lot and that thing was hard to miss. Glancing at his cart she noticed it was suspiciously empty.

She narrowed her eyes. "What are you doing here? Did you follow me?" Damn, why did he have to stand so close?

His sly smile was slow and easy. Fine laugh lines fanned out from eyes that glittered with mischief. His teeth were straight white, and there seemed to be so many of them. Was that an ever so slight hint of a dimple in his left cheek? Yeah, yeah it was. Holy Moses, the man was a wet dream walking and that smile was pure sin. He wore button fly jeans, God help her, and a black polo shirt with two buttons open.

He stepped closer, picked up the small cucumber she had selected for her salad and met her gaze. "Aw, Becca, this will never do, sugar."

"Huh?" she mumbled, momentarily distracted by thoughts of tasting his neck. "What?"

He lifted a brow. "This." He lifted the little cucumber. She stared at it frowning, shaking her head "Becca, this will never satisfy you, baby, not now anyway, not since the other night." Rebecca's mouth fell open and she stared at him, dumbfounded. He looked at it, pressing his lips together, and shook his head. "Nope, this won't do at all." He strode past her to the produce department and started searching through the sparse selection of cucumbers.

Rebecca shut her mouth with a snap. Fascination, disgust, curiosity and anger began to war in her mind, making her want to scream in frustration. She marched over to him and grabbed his arm in an unsuccessful attempt to turn him to face her. His bicep was round, tight and warm under the cotton of his sleeve. The contact was electric, although slight. He looked down at her hand then at her.

"Now you listen to me, Sheriff." Jerking her hand away, she spoke low, her voice trembling with rage and an overcharge of sensual awareness, which she chose to ignore. "I will never, ever sleep with you again. Do you understand me?"

He grinned. "Sure, sugar." He held up a long, round, smooth cucumber. "This one is damn near perfect."

Her eyes widened and she stammered a moment.

"Yeah, beautiful, isn't it?" He pushed it toward her at an obscene angle and she leaned away. "Feel how smooth…hard to find 'em that smooth and firm, too."

"It was for a salad…I wasn't…"She started shaking her head and backing up. "You're not…did you hear me?" She stopped. Shaking off the shock, she put her hands on her hips and glared at him. "I said…"

"Yeah, I heard what you said." He looked at her pointedly. "However, your body is telling me something else. "

"Teasing me won't work, Jackson."

"I haven't started teasing you yet, Becca, and already your cheeks are flushed pink with heat. So is your neck." He ran a finger down her neck to the hollow at her throat. "I love it when your neck does that and I'd be willing to bet my truck that your breasts are rosy, too. That love bite must be fading by now. That has to be remedied. Becca baby, I know they miss my attention; I can see your pretty nipples pressing against that cute little tank top. And those wildcat eyes of yours have already gone dark."

"Sheriff," she snarled in frustration. Closing her eyes, she pleaded softly. "You are making a difficult situation worse. So unless you have official business that requires my assistance, just leave me alone."

"Can't." He sounded almost regretful.

"Why?"

He gave her a sideways look. "Do you really want me to say it again? Here? In the middle of Piggly Wiggly?"

She pressed her lips together and stalked off. She rammed Jackson's cart out of her way and tried to remember what she came for in the first place. Oh, the arrogance, the audacity of the man! What appalled her most, what really pissed her off, was the fact that he was right.

She was aroused, the creamy hot slide of moisture between her thighs only added to her discomfort. And only from his nearness and his sexual threats. Yeah, she had to admit, he had her body aching for him, again. Dammit, did she have no control over her libido at all? It wasn't like she'd been with a lot of men. Jackson was her first one-night stand, ever, but she'd had several relationships and never had she been so easily affected.

He pulled his cart up next to hers in the dairy aisle and leaned across her, reaching for the whipped cream. His arm brushed her breast, sending an electric shock of sensation singing through her. "I'm following you home, Becca," he whispered close to her ear then put the can in his cart before reaching for another. "And we're gonna have a good time." She turned her head and happened to glimpse the contents of his cart. He still had the cucumber and had added a jar of chocolate sauce and bananas. He reached across her for one more can.

Rebecca held her breath, trying to rein in the urge to jump him. "Sweet tooth?"

He gave her a wry smile. Leaning down, he lightly kissed her mouth, lingering there for a moment. He flicked his tongue over her bottom lip before he moved away. "You have no idea." He ran the tip of his tongue over his top lip. "But I'm getting ready to take care of it." He winked at her and walked away.

* * * * *

Rebecca pulled into her drive and groaned as moments later Jackson pulled in behind her. She quickly hauled her groceries through her sparse living room to the small eat-in kitchen, aware that Jackson was right behind her. Rebecca set the sacks on the table and began putting their contents away in the cabinets. She paused, watching Jackson put his three cans of whipped cream in her refrigerator and she couldn't contain the snicker. She leaned back against the counter and covered her mouth with the back of her hand.

"What?" Jackson grinned.

But Rebecca just shook her head and laughed.

He moved to her, caging her in with his body. Oh, he smelled good and it felt good to laugh with him. The tension had been painfully thick all week. She smiled up at him and stifled a sigh. He was so damn gorgeous and he could do things to her that she'd never even thought to fantasize about. So why the hell was she fighting it? She reached up and touched his face. Her smile faded as their lips met. Gently at first, then the flash fire of need surged through her. She pressed her body to his, loving the hardness of his body.

"What's so funny?" he asked against her lips. She felt the bulge of his erection as he rubbed it against her stomach.

She smiled and met his dark gaze. "We can't eat three cans of whipped cream."

"Hmmm, well maybe not all at once, no." His lips left a trail of flames across her jaw to her ear as he nibbled slowly. "But it's nice to have it on hand. Just in case. It's a good idea to be prepared."

She put her hands on his chest and pushed him away. "Okay, Jackson, we have to stop. We can't."

"Mm hmm, we can, Becca, we did. I know you remember." He crushed her against him again and kissed along her jaw. "Let me refresh your memory." Taking his time, giving each inch his full attention.

"No listen, we need to be serious, just for a moment." She shoved him away again. Her voice had gone husky.

His hands gripped her waist and pulled her to him. He nuzzled the sensitive skin right under her ear. "I am serious, I'm fuckin' religious about this." His lips nipped at her neck and shoulder. "You're invading my dreams, Becca, and my nightmares. My dick hasn't been at ease since you walked those legs into the Wild Rose swinging that fine ass of yours." At some point, she wasn't sure when, he unbuttoned her shorts. His hands slid inside the waistband of her panties to cup her bottom. "So soft, round, firm. Fits in my hands like it was made for 'em," he murmured, pulling her hard against him.

"Stop," she whimpered weakly.

He pulled back and searched her face. "If you really want me to stop I will, Becca." He lowered his mouth to hers, his lips moving sensually over hers, his tongue stroking the delicate skin inside her lips then teasing her tongue. She wasn't thinking anymore. "Do you want me to stop? Do you?"

"No," she whispered harshly, pulling his shirt from his jeans, desperate to touch his skin. "To hell with it."

"Thank God," he said, grinning at her fervent struggle to get closer to him. He let her go long enough to pull it over his head. She couldn't wait, her hands glided over his warm body, the crisp chest hair tickled her palms, his nipples hardened at her fingertips and she sighed.

His erection was unmistakable and her body craved the feel of him inside her, stroking the very core of her. She fumbled with the button fly of his jeans. Her knuckles grazed his hard shaft, her frustration mounting.

"Jackson." Her strained voice seemed to come from far away; the sound of her blood pounding through her veins was so loud.

"Yeah, sugar?" His mouth was like a brand on her ultra sensitive skin and she momentarily forgot what she was doing. Her shorts and panties slid to the floor. His hands cupped her ass and continued to squeeze and rub as he pulled her closer. Waves of sensation unfurled from her core and feathered through her entire body. His fingers stroked the cleft of her bottom cheeks. His leg spread her thighs apart enough so that his fingers delved lower, slipping into her hot dewy channel then slowly circling the entrance with just enough pressure to have her moan breathlessly. Her blood surged hot through her veins to collect in her nipples and clit, causing them to swell with the need to be touched.

"You're burning me alive," she moaned. Finally unbuttoning the last button, she trailed her fingertips along the underside of his cock. Their mouths met again in a fiery tango of tongues and gasps. Rebecca pushed his jeans down, freeing him. Wrapping her hand around his shaft, her thumb passed over the ridge at the base of its pulsing plum-like tip. Breath hissed through his teeth and she kissed his chest, nipping at his collarbone and licking the hollow at his shoulder.

"Well then I'm goin' up with you." He pulled her tank top over her head and had her bra unfastened and on the floor before she could acknowledge what he was doing. Her breasts filled his palms; he lifted them, his fingers caressed them and squeezed her nipples. Pleasure sizzled along her nerve endings and they both moaned. He bent and took one hard peak between his lips and gently rasped his tongue over it.

Aching heat speared through Rebecca, her legs buckled and she wrapped them around his waist and groaned as the thick head of his cock probed at the sensitive wet folds of her heated cunt. She fisted her hands in his hair and rocked against him. He braced her body, trying to hold her still. She met his gaze. "Hurry." Her voice was low and sultry. She wrapped her arms around his neck and bit his shoulder with a growl then flicked her tongue over the spot.

"Wild cat," he hissed, carrying her to the bedroom. "I'm going to teach you the value of taking it slow if it kills me." He sat her on the bed, leaned down and kissed her quick on the mouth as he untangled her arms. "And it just might. "

He stood and stripped off his jeans. She looked up at him, her body vibrated, anticipating his touch. She couldn't help but smile at his hot survey of her body. This man made her feel like a goddess. She wanted to be the one torturing him this time. She wanted to see his eyes glaze over with the force of his climax. She shifted to her hands and knees and crawled down the bed to where he stood. She gripped his cock firmly when he tried to push her back. "Not this time, cowboy. You've gotten your way, it's my turn now," she said and trailed her tongue over the crease that led to the tiny opening. With a slow grin she watched him swallow hard.

"Wait, I..."

"Shhh, sit and lay back." She moved over him, as he did her bidding and urged him to slide higher up the bed. She continued lightly massaging his incredibly stiff erection but couldn't resist tasting the taut skin of his stomach. Warm spasms against her tongue tempted her lower. She heard his breathing accelerate as she scooted down to nestle his hot cock between her breasts. His breath caught and his hips pressed him closer. "Becca, baby, you're so soft."

She wished she had some oil on hand or something, she thought. Oh well, sometimes a girl has to improvise. She shifted and in one smooth stroke took him into her mouth as far as she could, making him as wet as she could with her saliva. Then secured the thick glistening shaft between her breasts again.

"Good God," he muttered as his hips rocked back and forth. Rebecca pushed her breasts together and bent her head to suck the tip as he slid smoothly between them. Heat infused her body, her inner walls clenched and erotic waves danced through her. "Oh yes, Becca, tighter, baby." She pressed her breasts tighter against his steel-hard cock.

Her mouth closed over the round head of his cock and drew him deeper into her mouth till she felt him throbbing against the back of her throat. She swallowed him deeper then moaned, the sound vibrating along Jackson's shaft. "Ah, yes," he groaned. She milked the thick ridge that pulsed along the underside with her tongue, pressing firmly as she sucked. His hands fisted in her hair and she thought she heard him growl. She caressed him with her lips as she glided up to lick and kiss the silky tip.

With one hand she cupped his balls and traced firm little circles on the patch of flesh behind them. Her tongue delved into the crease and she closed her lips over the tip, sipping at the pearl of arousal that collected there, and then surged over him again. He began thrusting into her mouth, his breath coming in pants. His muscles tensed as he gently rubbed his thumb over her cheek. "I can't hold back anymore, Becca."

She moaned against his flesh and sucked harder. His balls tightened. "Becca… Oh Jesus!" She took him even deeper and swallowed as his climax splintered and his hot seed spurted into her mouth. Her mouth pulled and milked him until he lay still, gasping for breath, his body coated with a sheen of sweat as she lapped up the last drop of his ejaculation.

He reached for her and pulled her into his arms. "You okay, sugar?" he murmured against her hair. His hand moved over her breast and she closed her eyes, drinking in the spirals of pleasure.

"Mm hmm." She laid her hand over his as it stroked her breast, teasing her nipple. She loved it when he did that. He slid one leg between hers and pressed his hips against her. Her eyes opened wide and she turned her face to him. "You're hard...again...already?"

"Mm hmm." His lips met hers in a tender caress. His tongue mated with her mouth. "It seems..." he kissed down her jaw, "that I can't..." nibbled her neck, licked her collarbone, "get enough of you." He adjusted his body till he was laying over her, nuzzling his face between her plump breasts, inflaming her skin with each flick of his tongue, each scrape of his teeth. The weight of him only added to her arousal. She raised a leg and thrust her hips forward, pressing against his hard thigh as his lips finally closed over one eager nipple. She cried out, her hands clutching his shoulders. "Sweet Becca," he moaned against her aching flesh.

She arched up, giving him better access. His hand slowly moved down her stomach to comb through the soft curls of her mound. She shuddered as he cupped her, dipped his fingers silkily into the drenched folds. "Jackson, please." She moved her body against his hand; the feel of his rough skin against her slick tender flesh almost sent her over. Then suddenly he took her wrists and placed her arms above her head, kissed her mouth and moved away from her. She shivered at the sudden chill and looked up at him grinning down at her.

"S'okay, sugar, I'll be right back. Don't move, don't go anywhere without me." He tilted his head downward and cut her a look. "I mean it, Becca, stay just like that. Don't move." He looked at her for a moment and took a deep breath. "You're so sexy like that. I'd handcuff ya if I didn't like what you do with those hands so much."

Rebecca watched Jackson's fine ass as he turned and walked out of the room. Whimpering, she took a deep breath of her own.

Chapter Twelve

Rebecca lay frustrated on the bed, her hands behind her head, her knees raised and swaying open and closed as she gritted her teeth and stared at the ceiling.

"I'm back!" She looked over to find Jackson standing in the doorway holding a cucumber. "Damn, I shoulda brought my camera!"

"Like hell!"

"Aw, Becca, it's a Polaroid. It'd be fun. And I'd have a picture of that pretty pussy anytime I wanted a peek."

"No, I mean the vegetable, Jackson."

"Well, technically, baby, it's a fruit." She gave him a look. He shrugged, looking down at the long fat cucumber. "Well, don't rule it out; let's just see how it goes."

She rolled her eyes. "Okay, can I move now?" He grinned and jumped on the bed. He leaned down and kissed her mouth hard and fast, then latched onto her nipple and sucked hard. "Oh, ow! Damn!"

The rumble of Jackson's laugh against her breast caused her to squirm closer. "I'm sorry, sugar. Let me make it better." He teased then laved her abused nipple with his hot tongue. Rebecca swallowed hard and looked at him.

She squinted at the cucumber in his hand. Its peel had been shaved away in a wide spiral design all over. "What did you do to it?"

"I decorated it." Jackson waggled his brows. "Makes for better friction." He turned it in his hand. "Did a good job, too. Ain't it pretty?"

Her eyes widened then narrowed. "What are you up to?"

He turned on his side, propped up on his elbow, and looked down at his erection. "I'd say we got almost seven inches, but Bubba'll get a little bit bigger as we go along."

She looked up at him with a grimace. "Bubba?"

A wicked grin slowly spread across his face and those steel gray eyes glittered with mischief. His palm idly rubbed over her breasts, teasing her nipples and then he trailed his fingers lightly through the valley between them. He winked at her and planted a kiss on her chin. "Yep. Bubba."

She gestured with a nod and turned toward him, pressing her breasts against him. He rubbed his nose against hers and kissed her mouth softly. Rebecca lifted a brow. "Won't Bubba be jealous of…uh…the jolly green giant ya have there?"

He frowned in feigned seriousness. "Naw, Bubba and me, we got an understandin'." She draped a leg around his hip and ran her hand up his back and down to squeeze the cheek of his rock hard ass.

"Oh yeah?" She reached between them and caressed him, tenderly stroking up and down.

His eyes darkened, their gaze sharpened. "Yeah." He leaned in and kissed her, his hand moving down to rub the wet curls that covered her mound, then dipped lower.

"What understanding?" she asked shakily.

"Play toys can be fun, a whole hell of a lot of fun. But when it comes right down to it, sugar, Bubba can not be replaced."

She tilted her head and kissed him deeply, sensuously. Arousal flowed through her like warm honey. "Hallelujah," she murmured softly against his mouth.

"Don't be too hasty now, baby. You're gonna love Mr. Cuke."

She laughed. "We shall see."

"Oh, hell yeah, we will." He moved lower and her body shuddered as he rubbed and sucked and molded her breasts, worshiping them. He caressed her ribs with his mouth. She was torn between arousal and ticklishness. Jackson chuckled at her squirming. He moved to her navel, his teeth grazing over the little dip. His fingers slipped between her lips and slid through the hot cream of her arousal.

He moved his fingers gently, slowly spreading her honey over her tender folds, her hardening clit. She arched into him. He kept teasing the soft skin below her navel with his tongue as he slowly inserted two fingers into her tight channel. She moaned, her stomach quivered. He laved lower still as he moved in and out, stimulating and stretching her clenching sheath. He moved around till he was between her thighs. "Scoot back, Becca," he said with a smile.

"Jackson, what are you going to do?" she asked. Feeling a bit nervous but excited, she moved higher on the bed to give him room.

He met her gaze. "I'm gonna make you feel good, Becca. Don't worry, I won't do anything to hurt you." He smiled and winked at her, comfortably positioning himself. He bent and flicked his tongue over her clit.

"Ah! Oh, okay, okay," she whimpered.

"That's it, sugar. Mmm you taste so good," he murmured against her. "Such a pretty, sweet, tight little pussy." He probed her again and ran his fingers around the slick opening of her vagina. "Just relax, Becca."

She nodded and bit her bottom lip. Jackson spread her legs apart until she was completely open to him. He nipped and licked at her inner thighs as he rubbed the cucumber through her juices and swirled it around her clit then probed her opening. She couldn't believe how good it felt. Her breath was coming in little moans. She couldn't help it. But when he leaned closer and took her clit between his lips, lightly drawing on it as he slowly pressed the cucumber deeper inside her, she thought she'd come apart. "Oh my God. Jackson."

"That's good, baby," he whispered, his hot breath on her, fanning the flame. His tongue circled her clit and he pressed deeper into her. She tilted up, thrusting against his mouth as his fingers slid down, massaging the sensitive skin between her vagina and anus. She cried out, tossing her head back and forth.

"Deeper, Jackson, go deeper." She felt his smile against her pussy and couldn't help smiling herself. "Oh yes." She arched up off the bed.

Jackson obliged her and licked from the cuke to her clit in hot firm strokes as he began moving the cucumber. Her cunt pulsed and clenched and she ground her hips upward to take more of the cucumber rasping in and out of her. His mouth latched onto her clit and he gently sucked on it. Her pussy began to vibrate but she was too close to orgasm to understand it. Through the deafening sound of her blood pounding through her veins she thought she could hear him humming. "Oh faster, oh, Jackson."

She moaned, her hands clutching at the sheets as he worked her with his mouth, his fingers, the damn cucumber. She cried out and bucked against him as her world burst into a myriad of color, her body trembling with the impact of her orgasm. She closed her eyes and rode the cucumber and Jackson's mouth until the hard spasms pounding inside her smoothed to soft pulses. Rebecca lay there as Jackson pulled the cucumber from her clenching body. He bent and laved her cunt. Lapping up her juices, his tongue speared into her then licked up to her clit. He drove her up again, torturing her with that incredible tongue. She fisted her hands in his hair and tried not to pull as she screamed his name through her next orgasm.

* * * * *

"I'm sorry I pulled your hair." She was stroking it back away from his forehead. His head lay between her breasts, his eyes closed. His dark thick lashes made him look so young. She kissed his hairline and continued smoothing a finger over his brow, making circles over his temples, and tracing the tiny lines fanning from the corner of his eye.

"S'okay, I'm hard headed." He smiled. His lips were full and firm and well defined. She nodded and smiled at that. "Hey, you didn't need to agree, I can feel your nod."

She chuckled. He sure was stubborn and strong and sexy and bold and fun. He was like no man she'd ever met. "I can't believe I fucked a pickle and loved it."

Jackson sighed and nuzzled her breast. "It was a cucumber, not a pickle. The Jolly Green Giant!" He opened one eye. "And, baby, it was *I* who fucked you, not the cucumber."

"Nope, doesn't count, you weren't inside me so it wasn't you. I was fucked by a...cucumber." She tried to contain her smile and feigned deep thought. "You know, I think cucumbers are a summer crop. I bet I still have time to plant some." She looked down at him with mock excitement. "Oh man, if I get me some Miracle Gro, there's no tellin' what I could produce!"

He opened both eyes and sat up. She lowered her eyelids, stared at the ceiling dreamily and moaned.

"Hold on here. It was me; I was the one, baby. In fact, I made you come hard enough to rattle your molars."

"Oh, please."

"Yeah, I think you said that too!"

"Sheriff Montgomery, are you feeling threatened by a cucumber?" She laughed.

"Hell no." He grinned. "I just think maybe you haven't been fucked good enough yet."

"Hmmm." She crossed her arms over her breasts. "Maybe not, then again..." She gave him a leveled look.

He scowled at her and, cupping her face, he captured her mouth with his. His hands moved over her, stirring the embers of her desire. He trailed kisses down her chin, to her chest, to the valley between her breasts. His hand lay on her stomach and inched downward but not far enough. He was teasing her, torturing her.

He moved back to her mouth and she could feel his smile against her lips. That did it. She rolled him over but he got the best of her by trapping her legs between his then locking his ankles over hers. His hot cock probed her mound and Jackson reached between them, directing himself between the triangle of her closed thighs and her tender folds. She groaned as his shaft glided over her swollen clit. His hands gripped the cheeks of her butt and passed his fingers softly over the cleft. She was going crazy. She wanted him inside her so badly she thought she'd die from the want alone. "Please, Jackson, I can't stand it."

He kissed her and stroked her hot mouth as he groaned surging his hips upward. The rough slide of his thick steely hardness wrapped in velvet as it speared through her creamy sensitive folds made her forget everything but her body and what Jackson was making her feel. Jackson looked up at her, his lids heavy over silver-ringed black pools of raw desire. "Yes you can, just hold on to me, Becca." His whisper was like a caress and her breath hitched.

Every cell strained for release but she struggled to hold back. Her hands clutched his shoulders and she lifted her chest from his, her nipples grazing his chest, exhilarating her, pushing her higher and higher. She pressed her pelvis closer, clenching her thighs, trying to keep him still. The head of his cock throbbed against her bottom. His palms pushed gently against her hips and he tilted his head back, driving up again. She saw stars; her climax was simmering there on the brink threatening to drown them both in the grip of pleasure. She was breathless, begging him, "Jackson."

Before she could think he flipped her onto her back. Jackson bared his teeth and with a growl, rammed his full, thick length into her to the hilt. Rebecca screamed as her orgasm exploded and she bucked against him, plunging upward to meet every thrust. The rippling waves barely had time to fade when she shattered again, the second climax sending her hurtling out of control as wave after wave washed over her. He rotated his hips, grinding against her with each thrust.

Driving her up again, Rebecca clung to his pistoning hips, clenching his cock tighter with her inner walls, pulling him deeper into her heat. She was so hot. She'd climaxed more than ever before and felt as though she would combust at any moment, but she wanted more, wanted it to last forever. He reached between them to torment the throbbing bud that ached for yet another release. Arching up, her moans turned to cries; her hands gripped his ass, urging him deeper.

Another orgasm shook her and she sobbed his name. Jackson's head fell back with a roar as his climax ripped through him. His body spasmed, filling her with each jet of his ejaculation, her greedy body milking every drop from him.

Chapter Thirteen

Rebecca awoke with a smile on her face. She stretched languidly, kicking the covers from her naked body without any modesty whatsoever. Her muscles ached, but it was a good ache. A nice hot shower would loosen them up. She curled her toes and sighed. Sex had never been this good, this fun. She felt like an overindulged feline and nearly purred with smug satisfaction. Opening one eye, she noticed the time on the clock and pouted. The cool sheets felt so good, but Jackson apparently had already left and she had less than an hour to get showered, dressed and be at the station ready to face whatever those two idiots decided to throw at her today.

She rolled onto her back and brushed the hair out of her face. The other hand she lay on her stomach. Jackson…he thought of him had her body humming. She closed her eyes and breathed deeply. What was she going to do about this sheriff? Her fingers trailed lightly between the valley of her breasts. She would have to talk to him; they had to cool off some if they were going to continue working together.

"Now see, that image is gonna haunt me all day long." Rebecca sat straight up and scowled. Jackson stood leaning against the doorframe with a wicked glint in his eye. He grinned and walked toward her, his voice was low and seductive. "Sorry, sugar, didn't mean to startle ya." He sat at the end of the bed and lifted one of her feet to rest against his shoulder and gently began massaging her calf.

"I thought you had left already." Her voice sounded breathy, her eyes fluttered closed as his hands moved higher, kneading the tight muscles there. He lifted her foot and she felt his teeth graze over the arch. Her breath caught in her throat as the sensation spiraled up and throughout her body. "You know we have to be at work, right?" she croaked softly.

He chuckled, that low sexy rumble. Was everything about this man hot? "I do, you have the morning off to rest. "

Watching him, Rebecca decided, who needed rest? He was tempting, dressed in those low-slung jeans and beige button down shirt. His sleeves were rolled up again, revealing his tight, tan skin over thick-corded muscles. She wanted him naked, covering her; she wanted that mouth all over her body again. Her vaginal walls clenched at the thought, the slick sliding between her thighs only added to her need. She couldn't get enough of him. Rebecca lifted a single brow and gave him a sly hungry smile. "I'm rested."

"Temptress," he growled at her and she nearly shivered. He moved over her and she reached up and ran her fingers through his shower-dampened hair. His hand cupped her breast. The heat of his palm, the roughness, sent delightful shivers racing over her skin. Her nipples contracted achingly for more attention and he obliged them, rubbing his thumb across their hardened peaks as he kissed her, swallowing her moan, his tongue playing with hers. He broke away too soon and nipped at her full bottom lip then licked it before moving away from her. "Gotta run, sugar." Jackson's voice was husky and she thought he growled when he bent and nibbled then kissed her shoulder.

She moaned seductively, watching Jackson's strong handsome face. His lids were lowered and with her free hand she cupped the growing bulge in his jeans. "Be late." Her hand moved over the outline of his thick shaft that pressed against the rough material.

His hand closed over hers as she started to unzip his pants. "Becca baby, you're killin' me." He cupped her cheek and kissed her. "I'd love nothing better than to stay in bed all day with you." He whispered. "But, I gotta go to work." He kissed her mouth once more then her nose. "You however, don't come in till one thirty."

"No, I'm scheduled for the eight to five shift," she said. Her obviously ignored pretend pout gave way to a frown. "I'm fine, I can do my job."

He moved away from her to the dresser, picked up his wallet and his gun. "I think you need to take the morning off, especially since you didn't go to the doctor and you've had a long..." he gave her a lascivious once over, "...eventful night."

Her eyes narrowed, "No more eventful than it was for you, Sheriff. Maybe you should take the morning off. I'm fine, I 'm fit and ready to rock and roll."

"Becca, don't argue with me on this. I have some business with the mayor this morning or you would have already tempted me to slack down on my responsibilities."

She sat up and swung her legs over the side of the bed. "I'm going to work."

"No, sugar, you're not. Now, you can either come in later or you can take the entire day off." He paused, meeting her gaze. She saw the resolve in those stubborn gray eyes and sighed, her shoulders slumped. "So you're coming in at one thirty. Hey, why don't you bring lunch by early...say eleven thirty or twelve? We'll have lunch in my office." He waggled his brows at her.

"Ah, no, I don't think that's a good idea. Look, Jackson, this...thing we've got going on needs to be kept private, for your sake and mine." He just looked at her and it unnerved her. He could not carry on his demonstrative affection for her at work. It would humiliate her, and it would ruin what tiny shred of respect she had earned from the other officers. "No really, Jackson. None of this." She waved her hand across an invisible line running between them. "Not at work."

He tilted his head to the side then to the other, "Alright, babe, we'll keep it a secret." He leaned over and kissed her hard and quick. "I put the coffee in a thermos so it'll be hot. Lie back down and get some rest. I'll see you at lunch." He turned to leave and, stopping with one hand on the doorframe, turned half way around. "Becca, I'll be thinking about you back here. Naked, hot, wet and those pretty pink boobs of yours with those sweet berries on top…" His eyes glanced over her body. "Mmm, God help me." He shook his head and left.

Rebecca couldn't go back to sleep, her body was too tense, wound up, hot. Damn him, she would pay him back for leaving her like this. A crooked smile curved her lips, and oh, how she would enjoy it. She stood and stretched again then walked to the bathroom and turned on the shower. She turned to the mirror and the woman smirking back at her looked positively wanton. Her cheeks were pink except for the ugly yellowish purple bruise fading over her right cheekbone. Her hair was a cloud of tangles. She licked her swollen lips; her heavy-lidded eyes were those of a woman with secrets…sexy, sinful secrets.

* * * * *

Jackson was feeling fine. Stepping out of his cruiser into the heat of a Tennessee summer, he inhaled deeply and fought the smile trying to tilt his lips. Today was a meeting with the mayor, and the man delighted in spoiling a good mood. Perhaps it was best not to let Whittaker know just how good his mood was.

"Afternoon, Jack," Margie Ferguson greeted him as he entered the mayor's outer office. "You look fine this morning. What has you so chipper?"

Damn, he wasn't pulling off somber as well as he used to. Margie was a bleached blonde, forty-something soccer mom with delusions of regaining her high school days. She wore the makeup heavy—especially the bronze blush, blue eye shadow and mascara—and she had thick, heavily permed hair. She was a good woman though, and damned near always had a smile for everyone. How she put up with Mayor Whittaker's sour attitude Jackson had never figured out.

"Morning, Margie, you're fine yourself. How's the mayor's mood this morning?" he asked her in a near whisper, smiling down at her slow and easy.

She rolled her eyes at the question.

"Figures." He grimaced, pretending to shudder. "Is he ready for me, or do I need to cool my heels a little longer?"

"He's ready, but he has company." She glanced toward the office to be certain of privacy. "Some slicked up city boy out of Detroit. Didn't we just get a new officer from there?" she frowned questioningly.

"Yep, we sure did." Jackson kept his expression bland. "So do I just go in or wait on my summons?"

Margie fought her snicker and lost.

"Go on in, you gorgeous thing." She waved to the door. "Just knock first. He yelled at his daughter for ten minutes for not knocking first."

Jackson shook his head. He strode to the door and rapped on the wood panel, perhaps a bit hard, as he concealed his smile.

"What?" Whittaker barked, obviously startled by the sound.

Hiding his smile, Jackson opened the door and stepped in. He kept his expression casual as he faced the mayor's curiously smug expression, and the oily superiority of the man with him.

The man was a pretty boy, there was no doubt about it. With his thick, sandy blonde hair just a bit long and brushed perfectly back from his long, arrogant face, thick light lashes and baby face, he likely turned a few female heads. He was built along the lines of a body builder rather than a man who actually put himself out to work, and carried himself like a reigning prince.

"Jackson, this is Todd Lawrence," the mayor introduced with the same officious pride of a man showing off his particular bright boy. "Todd, this is Sheriff Montgomery." Jackson assumed he himself was the dumb son if the distaste on the mayor's face was anything to go by.

"Lawrence." Jackson nodded as the man stood silently beside the mayor's desk. Hell, he wasn't about to offer to shake that snake-faced bastard's hand. They were staring at him like he just crawled out from under some slime rock.

"Todd's in from Detroit, here to see a friend of his. He stopped by here after he learned some disturbing news when he stopped by your office." Whittaker frowned in obvious disapproval. He would have pulled it off, too, if Jackson didn't see the smug sneer lurking in his expression.

"And that was?" Jackson arched a brow as he tucked his hands in his jeans pockets and regarded the newcomer.

"Seems there's some question of sexual impropriety in your office with that new deputy of yours we hired." Whittaker crossed his hands on top of his desk and assumed his most pious expression. "This is greatly disturbin' to me, Jackson."

"Me too." Jackson lifted his brows. First he had heard of it. "Who's being sexually improper?"

"Lawrence heard tell it was you, with that pretty little deputy you threw such a fit over. Sexual harassment is a might dirty way for a man to play because he disagrees with that little gal in his office."

Jackson didn't bother to hide his surprise.

"Just whom did Lawrence talk to?" Jackson asked darkly. "I assume I'm allowed to know."

Lawrence stepped forward. "I heard the rumors and I talked to Rebecca myself not three hours before. She's very upset over this, Montgomery."

Now Jackson was hard pressed to hide his incredulity. He knew that was a damned lie. Not three hours ago Miss Ree-Becca was all curled up next to him, warm and comfy.

"You will, of course, not harass Miss Taylor by questioning her over this. We want to minimize her embarrassment." Mayor Whittaker frowned at him heavily.

Jackson watched them both carefully.

"I think a resignation would be in order at least, Mayor," Lawrence suggested. "Rebecca has been through enough, so I don't think we should bring her into this—"

"Oh, I think maybe we should." Jackson stiffened his shoulders. He gave Whittaker a hard look. "I don't know what they hell you're up to here, Whittaker, but you didn't put me in that office, and you can't take me out. And I'll be damned if you'll run me out of it on some trumped up charge. Let's call Officer Taylor in here and see what she has to say." Especially considering he knew damned well they hadn't talked to her.

"Rebecca, of course, wants to cause no waves. She assures me she will press no charges if you leave quietly—"

"Mayor, do I look like a dumb redneck to you?" Jackson asked him coldly, staring into the man's surprised face. "Let me assure you, I'm not. And I doubt very much Officer Taylor told you shit. But I'll be more than happy to ask her about it first opportunity. "

Lawrence and the mayor exchanged a telling look. Of course they didn't want him checking into this.

"There's no need to be so profane," Whittaker objected with acute distaste.

"There's no need to be a liar either, but someone in this room is, and I assure you it's not me." He gave Lawrence a chilling stare. "Now you two better get your stories straight and stop playing footsie here. I know damned good and well you haven't talked to Rebecca, because Rebecca's not one to bald-faced lie. So I'd like to know what the hell is going on here."

"Lawrence?" The mayor was obviously uncertain how to proceed.

"Perhaps I haven't spoken to Rebecca," he bit out. "But I have spoken to your officers, Montgomery, and I know how you've harassed—"

Jackson turned on his heel and stalked to the door.

"Montgomery, you have not been given leave to walk from this office." The mayor's voice rose in anger.

Jackson gripped the doorknob, glancing back at them, anger churning in his stomach now — anger and a suspicion that ate at his sense of pride in his job.

"I don't need leave," he said, his voice harsh. "I don't know what the hell's going on here, but I intend to find out, you can bet on that. You want my job so damned bad," he sneered at Lawrence, "then come and take it, if you can."

He jerked the door open and then slammed it as he stalked out. Son of a bitch. He ignored Margie's look of shock as his boot heels thundered across the hardwood floor and the outer office door was given the same treatment as that of the mayor's.

He knew Whittaker had been trying to get him out of office ever since he took the position, but he hadn't expected this. This one had been more than a surprise. That the man would come at him with lies shocked him. On the other hand, his fists clenched, if his relationship with Becca hadn't progressed, then he would have likely been more than willing to believe it. His cynicism in most cases was well known.

Jackson was laid back, affable, but always silently suspicious. His trust in Rebecca shocked him for a minute though. He didn't really know her, she could have been there to play traitor, but he knew to his soul she wasn't. They were using her, and damned if that didn't make him madder than hell.

Jackson growled under his breath as he unlocked the car and got inside it. He needed to get back to the office and call Ted back. He needed another Detroit cop checked out now. At this rate, he was going to owe Ted a whole week away from Candy, and damned if that wouldn't suck. Candy was pure mean when Ted dropped her off for one of his hunting weekends. So mean that Jackson refused to let her stay last year. Damn, he hoped his ole buddy was in a gracious frame of mind when he called.

Chapter Fourteen

The morning off had done wonders for Rebecca. The hot pounding spray of the shower had her tight muscles yielding, leaving her feeling lithe and flexible again. She had put her hair up into a ponytail, shaved her legs and applied her makeup so that it nearly hid the bruise. At exactly 11:45 Rebecca swung open the station door feeling cocky and self-confident. Let the bastards show their asses today. She felt good, sated, ready to deal with anything, even a good ass kicking if it was warranted and she'd deliver it with a smile.

The station was only marginally cooler than outside and just as humid. Big metal fans blew dust around the small dim area. A coffee pot sat half full on an old metal cart huddled in the corner. Bryan made the best coffee and he always kept it fresh when he wasn't on patrol. If for no other reason, Rebecca thought, her transfer was worth that coffee. Bryan smiled cautiously up at her from behind the large metal desk facing the doors. It was as neat and orderly as Officer Matthews himself.

"Hey, Taylor, you're with me today." He grinned. "Uh, on patrol."

Rebecca grinned back. "Cool."

He blushed a little, his blond brows pulled together over those curious pale blue eyes of his. "Oh, and Sheriff said you were to come to his office as soon as you reported."

"Thanks, Matthews," she said without glancing back at him.

"I don't reckon it's anything to worry about though, I don't think he was pissed over anything," Bryan said following her down the hallway. "Sheriff seemed to be in a pretty good mood."

"That's good." *I'm sure he is,* Rebecca thought and couldn't help but smirk.

She turned into the locker room and noticing Officer Davis, chose to ignore him. She stuffed her purse into the locker and took her uniform shirt off the hanger.

"I was wonderin' if you was plannin' on puttin' some clothes on," Davis spat. Evidently he wasn't going to ignore her. It was going to be a hot day, she wished she could get away with the uniform trousers and white cotton tank top she wore into the station.

"Hey, I'd vote for tank tops on a day like today," Bryan piped up and laughed nervously.

Davis just shook his head with a derisive harrumph. "Yeah, I know what you're up to."

Rebecca shut her locker and locked it then turned on her heel. "All right, Davis, let's hear it. What am I up to?" She stood, hands on her hips, waiting for an answer. She could feel the anger rising but she kept her face placid.

He jutted out his jaw and glared at her. "All's you need to know is, I know, Martin knows. Hell, we all see through you, missy."

Rebecca tilted her head and narrowed her eyes looking at him like he'd just spoken Greek. "Davis, have you been drinking? What the hell are you talking about?"

"Hell no, I ain't been drinking. I don't disrespect my uniform." His gaze ran the length of her body and he smirked. "You just need to know we ain't gonna put up with it."

Put up with what? she thought. She clenched her teeth, deciding that arguing with this man was a waste of energy and time. "Oh yeah?"

"Yeah and we ain't a bunch of idgits you can just come in here and handle with a swing of your ass, either."

Rebecca's smile looked more like a grimace. She looked at him a while. "Look, Davis, if your libido can't handle working with a woman then that's your problem..."

"My libido ain't interested in anything a little slut like you has got!"

"Hey! Officer, that was inappropriate..." Bryan started forward but Rebecca put up a hand to stop him.

Her smile faded. There were so many things she could say. She wanted to get in his face and cut him to shreds with the words that were pounding in her brain for release. But instead, she walked away with a wave of her hand. "Whatever." *Stupid old man*, she thought.

She walked out, punching Bryan lightly on the arm as she passed him. "You eat lunch yet?"

"Nope, hey, you okay?"

"Matthews, it would take more than a crotchety old, insecure man to ruin my mood today. You wanna run by the Sonic when I get done in there?"

"That sounds good, sure." Bryan nodded and gave her a smile then started back to the front.

* * * * *

She stood at Jackson's door and changed her mind about tucking her shirt in. With a devious smile she undid the buttons she'd already done, swept her uniform shirt aside and plucked at her nipples till they pushed, hard and erect, through her thin bra and tank top. She didn't knock, she just turned the knob and sauntered into the office, shutting the door behind her.

Jackson looked up at Rebecca standing there, her uniform shirt swept back, her hands on her hips; her full breasts stretching the fabric of the tank top, nipples pressing forward, and forgot what he was saying.

"Uh, I'll call ya back. Yeah, uh huh. Bye." He hung up and stared at her with unmistakable admiration in his gaze as he stood and walked around the desk.

"Hey, Sheriff Sugar," she said in a sultry growl. That look in his eye made her think she might be playing with fire, nevertheless, she wanted to tease him. She wanted him to lose that iron-fisted control of his. She closed the distance between them in a few slow strides and pressed her breasts against him, raising her lips to less than an inch from his. "You wanted me?" she breathed.

His groan reverberated against her chest as his hand gripped the back of her head and his mouth closed possessively over hers. His other hand seized her ass and pressed her close, his hips grinding against hers. Her body ignited, instantly reacting to him on a primal level. His tongue plundered her mouth, stroking and teasing. He had turned the tables on her playful seduction with one kiss. Damn, she was always in over her head with him. Her breath quickened and her heart pounded in her ears. Before her sanity left her and she surrendered, she lifted her hands and shoved firmly against his hard chest. "Okay, stop, stop," she said breathlessly refusing to look up into his eyes.

"Just answering your question, sugar." His fingers slid down her cheek and lifted her chin till their gazes met. Sure enough, there was that Cheshire cat smile of his. Like he'd just caught the canary. She licked her lips slowly and his eyes narrowed.

She fought the need to strip him naked. He was so warm, his hands were always bordering on hot. She wanted them on her bare, aching breasts. She stifled a moan and lifted a brow, hoping sarcasm would cool her lust. "I was referring to the summons I received when I came in."

"Did you bring lunch?" His hand moved to her ribs, his thumb made slow seductive circles on the underside of her breast. His other hand was still on her ass, massaging her and moving lower. She swallowed and tried to block out the sensations he was causing to tighten and unfurl low in her stomach.

"No, we agreed to keep this thing between us a secret, remember? What would it look like if I came skipping in with a lunch basket?" She frowned at him. Frustration and arousal were making her snippy. She gripped his wrists and moved his hands, stopping their torment.

"If you want to keep this thing secret then you ought not come in here with your shirt open, tempting me with those juicy berries all ripe and ready to be plucked." Her scowl only prompted another grin from him. "Hey, that might be an interesting fantasy. You be Little Red Riding Hood and I'll be the wolf." Even his laugh was sultry. He waggled his brows at her again and she tamped down on the urge to smile.

"You know…" In an attempt to change the subject, she took a few steps back, sat in the chair facing his desk and began buttoning her shirt. "You really need to hire a secretary."

"Nah, we don't have enough work for a full time secretary. Besides, Bryan likes waiting up there like a lovesick puppy for Officer Becca Sugar to walk in and make his day." He gave her a pointed look and Rebecca couldn't resist.

"He's a sweetheart and one hell of a sexy man."

"He's no man, he's a boy," Jackson said incredulously.

"But he has a nice ass and loads of potential."

"He's green." His smile faltered, his voice lowered. Rebecca kept her expression as blank as she could.

"But oh so eager to learn." Rebecca wrinkled her nose and lowered her lids on the word "eager" and Jackson's frown deepened.

"You gonna raise him the way ya want him, huh?" he said with raised brows.

Rebecca shrugged. "That's the best way." She picked at a nail, trying to hide her smile.

"Problem with that, Becca Baby, is you don't know what you want." He pushed away from the desk and sauntered over to her chair, looming over her. "So see, after all that training and raisin' up, all you'd have is a worn out confused little boy and an unsatisfied Officer Becca."

Rebecca glanced up at him, meeting his hot gaze. "You think you know me, do you?" she whispered.

"Hell no." He leaned in closer till she could feel his warm coffee-scented breath on her lips. She couldn't look away, his eyes were dark and stormy and focused on hers. "You were a lot simpler to deal with when you were a pesky little love-sick girl. Hell, if I'd known then what I know now, I would have paid closer attention. Now that you're all grown up, I don't know half as much as I want to…as I'm going to." His flicked his tongue over her bottom lip. "But I do know enough to understand that you need more than a pretty boy with a nice ass to make you scream, Becca."

Rebecca scowled and shoved him away as she stood. She moved back and began tucking in her shirt. "You are so arrogant."

He took a step toward her, his gaze still locked on hers. "So are you."

She retreated a step. "Me?" Her eyes widened. "You're the one who has to feel like he's calling the shots."

He took another step toward her. "Yes, you, and I am calling the shots."

She retreated, feeling a bit off center, hot, irritated. "Maybe, but that doesn't mean you get to have whatever you want."

Slowly he stalked her. "I want the same thing you want, Becca." His voice was a near purr, pulling at her, making her want contact. The memory of the feel of his hot skin against hers flashed in her mind and she nearly gasped. She backed into the wall, his hands braced on either side of her head, and he pressed his body into hers. "God help me, I may want more."

"Jackson," she said softly, shaking her head. He moved against her, pressing his thigh between her legs against her mound. An explosion of sensation flooded her body. How could she be so aroused so quickly? She closed her eyes and bit her lip against the hungry moan clawing from deep inside her.

The knock at the door sounded like a gunshot and had almost the same effect on Jackson. He jumped away from Rebecca, his hand going to the weapon at his hip.

The door opened and Bryan popped in. "S'cuse me Sheriff...uh..." His eyes scanned the room from the desk to the bookshelves to his left. He blinked twice when he found them. Rebecca moved, her arms crossed over her chest, to stand in front of Jackson, afraid Bryan would notice the bulge pressing aggressively against the sheriff's fly. Jackson glared at Bryan, his hands on his hips. "Oh, hey, Sheriff, sorry to barge in...I didn't mean to interrupt...I mean."

"No big deal, Bryan." Jackson had meant to sound cool and casual but his voice was husky with arousal. "Just going over some things with Officer Taylor."

Bryan looked from one to the other and nodded, but Rebecca got the distinct impression that Bryan wasn't buying Jackson's statement. He stood, a bit fidgety, with a hand on the doorknob and cleared his throat. "Well anyway, shouldn't have barged in... Officer Taylor, you have a call. I explained that you were in a meeting with the sheriff and offered to take a message. But he seemed kinda insistent that he talk to you immediately."

Rebecca knew before she asked. "Who is it?"

"An Officer Todd Lawrence. He said he's a fellow officer from Detroit." Bryan's brows knit together as he watched her.

Rebecca stilled; her blood seemed to freeze in her veins. That asshole was never going to leave her alone. She gritted her teeth and nodded once. "I'll come take it." Before she could take a step she felt Jackson's firm hand on her shoulder.

"Just put it through to my phone, Bryan. You can take it in here, Becca."

"No, I think it would be best if—" Rebecca began.

"You can take it in here." His tone left no room for negotiation. Bryan frowned and backed out of the room.

Rebecca frantically tried to think of a way out as Jackson strode across the room to his desk. The short, shrill rings began just as he turned the phone toward her then sat back in his chair, crossed one leg over the other and folded his hands together over his stomach. She could feel Jackson watching her as she stared at the phone. She moved mechanically to the desk and picked up the receiver as she lowered herself to perch on the edge of the big overstuffed chair.

"Officer Taylor."

"Rebecca, sweetheart, it's so good to hear your voice."

Chapter Fifteen

Rebecca's stomach twisted and nausea swam over her. She wanted to scream at this man who didn't seem to understand the meaning of the word "no". If she could take back that year she'd spent with him she would. She'd moved four states away to try to be free of him, heal and move on. Now she sat here, avoiding Jackson's perceptive gaze as she listened to Todd's saccharine sweet endearments, and all the while refrained from exploding with rage. The image of Todd's face contorted in disgust, the threats, and the bruises he left on the surface as well as deep inside her, they were all still fresh in her mind. "Yes, Lawrence. What do you need?" She struggled to keep the fury out of her voice, her expression blank.

"Still so cold." He sounded as if she'd wounded him. God, he was infuriating. She grit her teeth. "Rebecca, I need to see you. We have to talk."

"No." It was simple, firm, clear.

"Rebecca, we will work through this. You've had enough time to calm down."

"Officer Lawrence, I'm on duty. Is there something job related you—?"

"You aren't alone are you, darling?"

"I can't see how that's relevant?"

"Rebecca, listen to me, sweetheart. I've heard things about the sheriff. Has he been harassing you?"

"That's not your concern, Officer."

"He has, hasn't he? Has he made a pass?" Rebecca's eyes widened and she glanced up at Jackson. In any other circumstance she would have laughed at Todd's asinine question. Pass, ha! He had no idea.

"Sheriff Montgomery has been a complete gentleman and as I said before, not your concern, Officer Lawrence."

"Oh, Rebecca darling, but you are my concern. I've heard that Montgomery has a reputation as a lady-killer. Be careful, I'd hate to see you get involved and get hurt." Jackson's eyes were cold and hard.

"Officer Lawrence, I can see no reason for you to contact me in any way. I was never your subordinate and am no longer of any consequence to you."

"Rebecca. I love you. Please, don't lock me out. I'm worried about you." He had softened his voice and injected just enough faux emotion to make her temper boil.

"Relax, Officer, I am perfectly capable of handling my affairs and dealing with assholes...as you well know. Now, if you don't mind I have work to do. So take your bullshit to someone who hasn't smelled the stench before." She slammed the receiver onto the cradle and worked on reining in her rage.

* * * * *

Jackson watched the fury that washed over Becca in silence. He narrowed his eyes as she took a deep, steadying breath, her breasts rising against the uniform top as she rose from the chair.

"You want to explain that?" he asked her carefully, his own anger rising.

His meeting with Mr. Pretty Boy Lawrence in the mayor's office hadn't quite lost its sting.

"How does he know about you?" She turned to look at him quietly.

Jackson watched the uneasy suspicion that entered her gaze as she stared at him. Her brows were knitted into a frown, her hazel-green eyes narrowed on him.

"What's going on, Jackson?"

Jackson sighed wearily, leaning back in his chair and watching her thoughtfully.

"I was called into the mayor's office this morning. I met your 'pretty boy' there."

Rebecca clenched her teeth. "He's not my 'pretty boy,' Jackson. Don't pull that shit with me now." He lifted a brow and held her gaze. "What did he want?"

"He tried to convince me he had talked to you this morning and you were accusing me of sexual harassment," he stated calmly.

Jackson watched the shock that flashed over her expression. Her eyes widened, her face paled.

"He didn't?" she gasped.

"Oh yes, sugar, he did." He grimaced. "And in the next breath demanded that the mayor demand my resignation from office."

Rebecca collapsed in the chair beside his desk. She didn't take her rounded, bemused eyes off him. Her mouth was parted, and the pale features began to flush with anger.

"That son of a bitch," she bit out. "Why would he do something so stupid? Did he think you wouldn't ask me about it?"

Jackson rubbed his chin. "Well, honey, to be honest, if I wasn't curled up nice and tight with you about the time Lawrence said he talked to you, I might have been pissed enough to doubt your word. I'm not a real trusting type."

Her eyes widened further in mocking amazement. "Are you telling me you wouldn't have at least asked me about this?"

"Eventually." He shrugged. "Thing is, people know about the night we left together at the Wild Rose. There's already talk somewhere, because a friend of mine heard it, and evidently the mayor has as well."

Rebecca groaned. She laid her head on the table, covering it with her arm as she shook it in slow denial.

"This isn't happening," she mumbled despairingly.

Jackson grinned. He couldn't help it. She was just so damned pretty.

"Well, sugar, I can understand his desire to get you back in his bed, but his means leave a lot to be desired here. And problem is, he's here now, and it didn't look like he was going to leave any time soon. Unless I miss my guess, him and our dandified little mayor are just a little too tight to suit me." Hell, they acted like damned bosom buddies.

"This doesn't make sense." She shook her head. "Why would he want to lie, or even care if you resigned? Why would he even be here?"

Jackson shrugged. His earlier conversation with Ted only added to his misgivings. Todd Lawrence was already under suspicion in his own precinct. Moving to some small town and weaseling his way into the department could just be a career move on his part. The fact that he was aligned with the mayor, who was aligned with Deputy Martin, had his radar going crazy.

"Is Lawrence a dirty cop, Becca?" Jackson asked her straight out. She was so furious with the man that it made him wonder.

Rebecca sighed and blew out a hard breath.

"He's a dirty, rotten, scumbag of a man." She shook her head. "I don't know if he's a dirty cop or not. He never gave that indication to me."

"How well did you know him?"

Rebecca flushed, shrugged.

"We were lovers for a year. We got engaged, I lived with him. But I can't say it was the happiest year of my life. Todd's not easy to get along with." Her hesitation had him frowning fiercely.

"Did he hit you?" Jackson knew he would kill the bastard if he had.

"Once," she bit out. "But there are worse ways to hurt a woman, Jackson. He was demanding and very vocal in his disappointments. Our relationship was one battle and one lie after another. He cheated and lied, and undermined everything I tried to do. No, he didn't hit me. But I could have handled that. It would have been easier."

He heard the confusion, the hurt that resulted from the relationship, in her voice. He fought to keep his expression bland, merely curious, but it was damned hard not to growl in possessive fury. The bastard had dared to hit her. He clenched his fists, raging silently and vowing that no one, ever again, would hurt her like that.

"Well, sugar, your taste is definitely on the upswing since you came home. I gotta commend you on that." He patted her arm, keeping his voice comforting and saccharin sweet.

"Oh, you think?" Her voice rang with exaggerated offense. "Dammit, Jackson, you don't have an opinion of yourself, do you?"

He leaned back in his chair, lowering his eyelids as he watched her, allowing a knowing smile to tip his lips.

"Tell me Mr. Cuke and Bubba wasn't just the best experience of your life, darlin'?" Come to think of it, it was the best-damned experience of his life, for sure.

She flushed, her cheeks turning rosy, her eyes darkening with remembered arousal.

"Conceited," she bit out. "You are so conceited, Jackson, it's not even funny. I don't remember you yawning with boredom when 'Bubba' was seated to the hilt in my mouth." Bubba responded as if he'd heard his name at the memory of her hot wet mouth wrapped around him, sucking, milking him for all he was worth... Damn. Rebecca smirked as if she knew the impact her words made on him. "Better watch out, hon, someone might knock you on your fine arrogant ass one of these days."

"Done happened," he told her, unconcerned. "You own my ass, Becca, you just don't want to admit it yet."

Hell, he hadn't wanted to admit it until Mr. Fancy Pants made his appearance.

He had shocked her. Her eyes widened.

"Okay, time for me to go to work." She jumped to her feet, checking her clothes quickly, avoiding his eyes.

"Coward," he accused her gently.

"Oh yeah." She nodded, heading to the door. "You know it, Jackson. Catch you later. Maybe you and Bubba can show me what you do for an encore after work."

Damn, that woman was never short of a smartassed remark. He watched her escape his office quickly, his cock throbbing, his chest tight. This Todd Lawrence thing could become a problem. A damned big problem if the bastard didn't stay away from Jackson's Sugar.

Chapter Sixteen

Driving around in the patrol car was making the day drag, and boredom was giving way to thoughts and memories Rebecca would rather not dwell on. Todd wasn't going to leave her alone. She couldn't believe he would follow her across four states. Did he take so much pleasure from making her miserable that he just couldn't let her go? And what was he up to? He had never heard of Jericho, Tennessee before she got reassigned. She never mentioned it.

Damn, she wished she could have kept the whole transfer a secret altogether. Who was she kidding? Even if they hadn't thrown the party and teased her about her country roots, Todd would have dug and dug until he found her. If she didn't know that before, she knew it now. What was most disconcerting was that he already knew about Jackson and he went straight for the man's jugular like a rabid dog.

Jackson... What was she going to do about that man? A sly smile flitted across her lips as she slid into the assigned cruiser. Everything in her wanted to sink her hooks into him and never let him go. He'd made her laugh; she hadn't even known she needed that, and he made her feel wonderful, strong, incredibly feminine, and God help her, she was falling for him. The scary thing was that she didn't give a damn. It made her hot just thinking of his hands, his mouth, his tongue...

"Hey." Matthews gave her a questioning glance. "You okay?"

"Hmm? Oh yeah, fine." Rebecca leaned down and turned the air up.

"I guess being on patrol in Detroit is a lot more exciting, huh?" he asked.

"I don't know if I'd call it exciting. It can get boring too, in a different way." Detroit seemed a world away now. A world she was thankfully no longer a part of.

"Yeah, that makes sense." He nodded then pointed to the road ahead. "Hey, turn up here and we'll work our way around and back to the station."

"Cool, shift's almost over anyway." Rebecca turned onto the narrow two-lane road. "It's been a slow day."

"Yeah, I'm hoping to get Jack to let me off a little early." He rubbed his hands together.

"Hot date?" She grinned, keeping her eyes on the road.

"Man, I hope so," he said, smiling sheepishly.

Rebecca laughed, and then her smile faded as the camper in front of them weaved a bit. "How long have we been following this rickety camper?" she asked, getting frustrated with the ten miles under the speed limit she was forced to drive.

"Not too long, they probably noticed us and they're bein' cautious." He shrugged.

Rebecca's brows knit together. "A bit too cautious," she murmured and straightened in her seat.

"Aw, you know how people get when a cruiser is behind 'em," he smirked, cutting his eyes to her.

"Yeah, but I get a bad feeling about this one." Rebecca's frown deepened. This was definitely not good.

It wasn't too much longer before the camper began to weave again. Maybe the driver was just tired, but she had a feeling either they were drunk or worse, nervous. "I'm gonna pull them over and check them out," Rebecca said, hitting the lights.

"Okay, guess it wouldn't hurt." He shrugged again, watching the camper closer.

The driver in the camper seemed to ignore her for a while. She doubted they didn't see her. She hit the siren in short bursts twice, then again. Finally they pulled over.

"Now, Rebecca, don't go in with a ball-bustin' attitude. Rednecks tend to rebel against that kinda thing. Hell, maybe I should go deal with it?"

She gave him a sideways glance. "Sheesh, Bryan, give me a little freakin' credit. I've been a cop for a while, I've even pulled people over before." There was a little bite in her sarcasm. "I know how to talk to people, regardless of the color of their necks…"

"Yeah, but…" He looked at her dubiously. "You ain't dealt with many rednecks yet."

"Ha! Are you kidding? I grew up with rednecks. And now I'm surrounded by rednecks!" she snapped. She was sick to death of being second-guessed.

"Rebecca, don't get mad, I'm just…" He gave her a worried puppy dog look and his shoulders slumped.

Good grief. "Look, Bryan." Her voice softened a bit as she reached for her ticket book. "Don't stress, I got it. Just call in the tags."

She rose from the car. She kept her hand on her gun and walked up to the cab cautiously. The driver rolled down the window. "Is there a problem, Officer?"

"License and registration, please." She kept her voice firm and authoritative as she leaned down and took stock of the driver and his passenger. Both were Caucasian males, clean-cut in jeans, clean shirts and baseball caps. The driver was a bit larger than the passenger. She guessed he might be six feet, tough looking but not all that muscular. The passenger was a bit over six feet and wiry. She didn't smell any alcohol on the man's breath or in the cab and he seemed to be coherent. However, his movements were jerky, his shaky smile and nervous chuckle alerted her that something wasn't right. The passenger fidgeted and wouldn't look at her.

"What'd we do, Officer? I was under the speed limit," he said, reaching for his wallet.

"I noticed you were weaving quite a bit..." A muffled cry had Rebecca stopping mid-sentence. She tilted her head to the side and raised a hand for the driver to keep quiet. "What was that?"

The driver looked up at her with wide eyes, his lips stretched into a tight smile. "What?"

Again she heard a whimper coming from the back of the camper. The sound was one of distress, fear. Was that a baby? It had the tiny hairs on the back of Rebecca's neck standing on end. There was definitely something going on. She turned to the driver in time to see his passive expression turn into a pinched, hateful snarl of a man desperate for escape. Rebecca had no time to react. The man swung open the car door, smashing the metal window frame against the side of her head.

White light exploded in her brain and she stumbled back. The camper wheels spewed dust and gravel as they sped away. Rebecca got up as fast as she could and ran back to the cruiser. Her head hurt and her stomach roiled as she jumped in and took off after the camper.

"Hey, hey, we're getting in over our heads here." Bryan watched Rebecca with wide eyes.

"Call for back up," Rebecca bit out. She blinked twice, the winding road in front her stopped undulating but it didn't help that it kept on curving up and around, as though it had been carved through the mountain by a snake.

"Rebecca, turn around. I got the tags; we'll go back to the station and report it. Let 'em go!" His voice was thin. His eyes darted from the road to Rebecca.

"Call it in, Bryan, we need back up." Rebecca's eyes narrowed as she struggled to keep the road in front of her in focus.

"No, no, we don't know what we're dealing with here, back off, Rebecca. It's too dangerous," he pleaded with her.

The tires squealed in protest as Rebecca made the next curve a little too sharp. Bryan sucked in his breath and grabbed the dashboard. "You don't know these roads, Rebecca. Pull over, and let me drive."

She clenched her teeth. "I thought you said this road takes us back to town."

"It does if you turn around at Melvin's Food and Gas back there." His voice was thin and a bit high-pitched.

"Shit, we need back up, call for back up. Where does this road take us?" She sped up and clenched her teeth against the pain clawing at her brain.

"Eventually into the Allegany Mountains of Virginia." He sounded panicky now.

"Shit! Call for back up, Bryan!" She yelled.

"Rebecca, you probably have a concussion, we can't, we…" Bryan turned in his seat, trying to convince her.

With one hand on the wheel, Rebecca grabbed Bryan by his shirt and yanked him closer. Her voice was low and menacing. "Officer Matthews, either call for fucking back up or I'm slowing down and shoving you out! Do you understand me?"

Bryan cursed under his breath and buckled his seatbelt tighter as he grabbed the radio mic.

Rebecca concentrated on her driving. Thankfully, her eyesight was steady and sharp again, although the siren only intensified the pain throbbing in her head. She heard Bryan's uneasy voice as he spoke with the dispatcher but his words didn't register. She kept her eyes focused on the curve of the road and the vehicle ahead. The camper shimmied and swayed all over the road. So far there had been little to no traffic. But, there was a child back there. Was he kidnapped? Was he hurt? How could she back down? She just had to stay with them until her back up showed.

She saw the glint of the sun on the barrel of the rifle just in time. "Shit! DUCK!" she screamed and pushed Bryan down in the seat just as a bullet punched through the windshield over Bryan's head.

"Stop! Stop now, Rebecca!" Bryan pleaded with her frantically.

"Just stay the fuck down!" Rebecca was pissed now—no, past pissed, she was livid. No way would she let the bastard go now. Bryan just barely missed catching the bullet with his face. She pushed the thought aside; she'd deal with that later. She had to catch these assholes. Bryan was speaking frantically into the mic again. She slammed her foot down on the accelerator and yelled in rage as a bullet hit her radiator.

"Rebecca!" Jackson's voice was clear and strong and it was the first time he'd said her name correctly. She grimaced, surprised that she didn't like it. "Back up is on its way. Can you maintain pursuit?"

She snatched the mic from a wide-eyed Bryan. "Affirmative, Sheriff. Too close to back off now. I think there's a minor involved," she replied, strangely calm even though she could feel her heart in her throat. The danger was very real, her career was on the line but so was the life of a child.

There was a pause before the radio crackled again. "Don't get headstrong and careless, Becca. Keep a safe distance."

A bullet shattered her side view mirror with a loud metallic ping. "No, sir, we can't lose them. I'm staying on them until I get back up."

If she let them escape they may never find them again. She'd been on the force long enough to know that, and Jackson knew it too. Grotesque scenes of what they might do with the child kept playing over and over in her mind, scenes of molestation, mutilation. She couldn't let them go, she couldn't.

"Dammit, Officer Taylor, was that gunfire? I heard gunfire." Jackson's growl crackled from the speaker.

She didn't have time to argue. "Just get me my back up, Sheriff." Gritting her teeth against the need to heave, she dropped the mic. Bryan picked up the mic and started to sit up. "No, Bryan, stay down. Just stay down, one less target."

Panic rose in her and clawed at her throat as she leaned into the steering wheel. White billows of steam were pouring out from under the hood and the car was loosing momentum. She could barely see through the web of cracks in her windshield and bullets still popped and pinged against her cruiser. God, she didn't want to lose them. It sounded like an explosion and for a moment she thought they'd go up in flames before she realized her right wheel tire was shot out. She braked slowly but the car was going too fast. It shook hard and bore to the right. She swerved, fighting for control, but lost the battle when the tire hit the soft shoulder. The scream sounded like it came from far away as the car bucked and flipped.

* * * * *

She didn't know how long it had been. She heard the sirens in the distance, the static of the radio and fuzzy voices. Pain seared through her head but she opened her eyes. "Bryan...hey, Bryan, you okay?"

Just turning her head had sickening spasms of pain pounding inside her skull. Bryan lay motionless. She had lost the child, the baby. They got away and Bryan was dead. He had to be dead. "Bryan," she cried out, fighting the darkness that threatened to envelope her again.

"Becca." She felt hands on her face, Jackson's hands, his voice. He was saying something she couldn't understand. "Stay with me, sugar."

Why would he say that? Confusion fogged her mind. She tried to look at him but the light sent shards of pain spearing through her head. "Jackson? The baby..." She felt herself fading back, darkness closing her off.

Chapter Seventeen

"God. Becca." Adrenaline and fury surged through Jackson as Becca collapsed in his arms, her last thought that of the child she had been unable to rescue.

He was terrified to move her from the vehicle, and could do nothing but check to make certain none of her injuries were life threatening as he heard the ambulance sirens in the background.

"Roby, check Bryan," he ordered as he watched the other office move around the front of the vehicle.

He barely caught the other man's expression of distaste. Jackson watched the officer carefully then, a surge of hated suspicion running through his gut. The other officer did as he ordered, though, checking Bryan's condition quickly.

"Gunshot wound to the shoulder, looks like a broken arm to go with it and he's out cold. He'll live." There was little sympathy in the other man's voice.

"Get Martin. You two get the hell out of here and see if you can find that truck. The State Troopers can assist me here."

"Troopers?" Roby jerked alert then. "Hell, Jackson, since when do we want Troopers in our business?"

"Since we have two officers down and the bastards got away." Jackson gave the other man a fierce, level stare. "Now get to it or you and Martin both can take a leave of absence while I find someone willing to follow orders."

Roby's lips tightened. Carefully, as though he were more than aware that Jackson was just looking for an excuse to tear him apart, he moved away from Bryan.

"This is a mistake, Sheriff," he muttered, his eyes narrowing on Jackson.

"Then it's my mistake, isn't it? Now get the hell out of here." He moved away from Becca carefully as though preparing to back up the order with action if need be.

Roby's fists clenched, he shook his head with a short, rough movement then stalked away. Jackson moved back as the paramedics rushed to the car, but he kept his eyes on Roby and Martin. After a brief, furious discussion, the two men moved quickly to their vehicle and headed away.

Jackson jerked his cell phone from his hip, watching the paramedics closely as they helped Becca and then Bryan from the wrecked car. He hit speed dial, then waited impatiently as the phone rang.

"What do you need?" Jacob's voice came across the line, quiet and controlled.

"You heard?" Jackson knew the other man kept a police scanner on hand, and there was no way in hell to block him from transmissions.

"I heard." There was a low throb of anger in the other man's voice.

Jackson knew if there were two things Jacob hated, then it was flesh runners and drug runners, and from all appearances, the ones operating in Jericho were more dangerous than most.

"Check your end, but don't get into trouble. They were headed that way. I sent Roby and Martin out after them, so be on guard."

Jacob grunted sarcastically. He was a man of few words when the situation warranted it.

"Keep your cell on hand," he finally growled. "I'll be back with you later."

"You do that," Jackson bit out. "And watch your ass. I don't have time to haul you out of trouble."

He disconnected the line as two State Troopers roared into the area, sirens blasting. A tight, cold smile shaped his lips as he identified the offers. Ted had come through for him. Jackson may be short on loyal deputies, but by God, Ted had just pulled two of the meanest damned Troopers to ever ride a Tennessee highway in to help him after his earlier phone call. His brother-in-law evidently wasn't taking any chances. These men were Troopers with a grudge, and the power to back up any investigation they undertook. Sandor Kylie and Gray Jensen.

He caught Sandor's gaze immediately. Tall, controlled, his hawkish look immediately taking in the scene. A brief nod was all the answer he needed. Assuming expressions of arrogant intent, the two officers strolled his way. Let the games begin, Jackson thought as the paramedics loaded Becca and Bryan into the ambulance, because it was about to get hot.

"Sheriff Montgomery." Sandor tipped his hat back on his head and surveyed the scene with predatory interest.

He was as tall as Jackson, lean and muscular, with a square jaw line, and piercing hazel eyes. He had once been more laid back and easygoing than he was now, but circumstances had changed that over the years.

Jackson was aware of the interested gazes of several off-duty deputies who had arrived to help with the scene. Men the mayor had hired. Men Jackson didn't trust, and he knew full well that his uncle hadn't trusted them.

"We got a line on your tags, and your boys," Kylie told him quietly as they moved along the end of the wrecked cruiser to assure privacy. "Truck was stolen 'bout two weeks ago. The witness described Jasper Michaels, a small time illegals dealer, as the thief. Jasper was seen not long before that with Wago Darney, an illegals flesh peddler of the worse sort. If you've tagged him and your officer saw him, then you best watch her ass. Wago doesn't like witnesses of any kind."

Jackson's jaw clenched. This was getting deeper than he could have ever suspected.

* * * * *

Bryan had sustained a concussion, broken arm and collarbone, and a wound to his right shoulder from the bullets fired from the vehicle they had been chasing. Rebecca had a concussion, sprained muscles, and a minor laceration to her forehead. Both officers had been surprisingly lucky, which only pissed Jackson off further. The bastards in that truck had meant to kill them both.

He paced outside Rebecca's hospital room the next day as she dressed. The doctor had released her, but had stipulated that she be off work for at least a week. With Bryan still hospitalized, Jackson was realizing that he was now surrounded by whatever conspiracy Mayor Whittaker and Todd Lawrence were involved in. It didn't help a damned bit to know that he should have suspected it before Rebecca's presence on the force.

"I'm ready." Rebecca walked from her room, dressed in the soft gray sweat pants he had brought, and a loose, light gray T-shirt. She looked tired and worried, and he didn't blame her. "Were you able to get anything on that vehicle?"

He tossed her a sideways glance. "You are on leave, Rebecca. No business for you for the next week."

Jackson took her arm as they walked to the elevators at the end of the hall.

"Jackson, I can't just lie around for a week…"

"Like hell you can't." He almost winced at the controlled violence in his voice.

Dammit to hell, he could have lost her. He almost shuddered at the thought. He was doing better, though; he had trembled for hours the night before as he waited to see how seriously she was injured.

"Jackson, you weren't the one who heard that child cry out," Rebecca bit out as they entered the elevator and Jackson hit the down button. "I was. That was a child in pain, and I won't just forget about it."

"I'm not asking you to forget about it," he told her, fighting to keep calm. "But you can't do anyone any good right now, Becca. Especially that child. Get better, maybe by then I'll have a lead on what's going on."

He was working on it, that was for damned sure. In doing so, he was realizing the problems he was potentially facing. He couldn't trust Roby and Martin. No way, no how. With Becca and Bryan out of commission, that left no one on his immediate force to back him. He had phone calls and plans to make, because he would be damned if he would see his county used for what he was suspecting it was being used for, especially by men who had sworn to protect it.

Silence lay between them then, thick and heavy, as he led her from the hospital entrance to the cool comfort of his pickup. He helped her in gently, then locked her seat belt in place and closed the door. As he walked to his side of the truck, he kept a careful eye on the cream colored sedan that had followed him to the hospital earlier in the day. He would have been worried, except the two men who watched him did very little to hide their presence and screamed Feds. Now why the hell would Feds be on his tail?

"I want to take you to my place," he finally told her as he pulled out of the hospital parking lot and headed back to Jericho. "We'll swing by your place and pack what you need then head to my house. I don't want you alone right now. Especially with Mr. Slick roaming around town."

"Who?" Her exclamation of surprise had him tossing her an irritated glance.

"Lawrence," he bit out. "He's been to your house twice since yesterday morning, according to your neighbors. I don't know what the hell is up with him, Becca, but I don't like the games he and Whittaker are playing. Our best bet right now is to keep you the hell away from him until we know what's going on."

He glanced over at Becca, watching as she licked her dry lips nervously. His cock twitched. Dammit, he really liked the sight of that. He wished he were the one licking those tempting curves instead, though.

"I really do not want to deal with this," she sighed, leaning her head back against the seat.

She was pale, bruised, and in no condition to be doing anything but sleeping, Jackson knew. She had demanded her release when the doctors would have kept her another day. Jackson had allowed it, simply because he knew he could protect her, if protection was needed.

Chapter Eighteen

"Dammit, Jackson, I'm not going to bed." She stood stiffly in his sparsely decorated living room. She scowled at him and sat on the sofa, her arms crossed, trying to hide the weakness she felt. "I'll sit here for a while." She nearly sighed; the big overstuffed sofa was plush and so very comfortable.

She looked up into Jackson's eyes and resisted her desire to cringe. They were hard and cold as granite. The muscle in his jaw flexed. "Rebecca. You fought me at the drug store when I asked you to take your pills and you took your pills. You fought me at your house when I told you to stay in the car. You stayed in the car. You fought me downstairs when I carried you up the steps. We already know I'm going to win. Stop being so damned bullheaded." He was mad and struggling not to yell. She could tell, but she couldn't seem to care.

"I'm not the bullheaded one. I will not lie around for a freakin' week. I'm gonna sit right here till this blasted pill wears off then I'm gonna kick your damn fine ass."

"When you're up to it, my ass is yours. Until then you'll damn well do what I say." His voice was low and menacing.

He picked up the suitcase he'd packed and walked down the short hallway. Damn man, she thought. She ran her hands through her hair and took a deep breath. She was starting to feel better. The pain wasn't as sharp and she was feeling warm and mellow.

She scowled in frustration and defiance as she glanced around, taking in her new surroundings. It figured, Jackson's apartment looked like the typical bachelor pad. The walls were stark white; no art or pictures were hung. Along the wall beside the front door was an oak entertainment center with a huge television and a really nice stereo system. A recliner sort of divided the living room from the dining area. The camel-colored sofa sat on the opposite wall from the entertainment center. A newspaper, two remotes and a Sports Illustrated decorated the coffee table.

Jackson returned with a pillow and blanket. Rebecca watched him warily as he dropped his bundle on the floor beside the sofa. He stood over her, his long muscular legs straddling her knees. Yummy. Her eyes dropped to his hips, the evidence of his arousal clearly straining against tough denim, just at her eye level. She raised her gaze to his and lifted a brow.

Jackson's eyes narrowed. "Don't look at me like that," he growled and began pulling her shirt up. The corners of her lips tilted upward as she cupped that hard bulge in his jeans. He held his breath and grabbed her hand. "Becca. You need rest."

She shook her head; it felt so heavy she leaned it back against the sofa. She didn't fight him as he undressed her and pulled her nightshirt over her head. "I don't need rest," she murmured, frowning. Her voice sounded weird. "I need sexual healing."

"Rebecca, baby." Jackson's voice sounded far away and so gentle.

"Hmm?" She reached for him. His mouth, she wanted that wonderful hot mouth of his on her.

"Go to sleep." He lifted her a bit to lay her down.

"I'm not laying down, Jackson. I don't wanna lay…around." She fought it but her eyes drifted close.

He kissed her forehead, her nose, her mouth. Just a tender kiss, lingering for only seconds. "Okay, Pixie, whatever you say."

* * * * *

Rebecca woke the next morning with a pounding headache. She opened her eyes slowly, and then squinted against the sunlight, hissing as she struggled to sit up. She scanned the room remembering where she was. Another blanket was thrown over the recliner. Coffee, she smelled coffee. She could see Jackson through the window in the wall that divided the dining area from the kitchen. He was making coffee... Follow the coffee, she told herself. Standing took more effort than she thought it should have. She had expected the pain to be bad and knew it would only be worse tomorrow. Lifting her chin she took a deep breath, she could take it.

Jackson saw her hobbling toward the kitchen, cursed under his breath, wiped his hands on a kitchen towel and helped her to a dining chair. "Becca, you need to be in bed. If you weren't so damn stubborn you wouldn't be as stiff."

She scowled at him. "Bullshit," she grumbled, thankful for his hard body to lean against. "Please, Jackson, I need coffee and Ibuprofen."

The man was fast and oh so efficient. She held her mug with both hands, inhaling the mouth-watering aroma of freshly brewed coffee. He set a glass of water in front of her and held a large white pill out to her in his wide palm.

"Take this," he said in an adamant tone.

She looked at the pill. "That's not an Ibuprofen."

"No, it's a Vicodin," he said firmly, lifting a brow. His lips were pressed together in a determined line.

"That will make me goofy. I need to get back to work." She turned away from him and sipped her coffee.

"Rebecca." He was warning her and it only made her more determined.

"I don't need it." She turned her head, careful not to grimace in pain, and met his gaze. "Quit treating me like a child."

"You're acting like a child," he bit out. "You take everything as a challenge."

"Whatever." Now he'd gone and pissed her off. She turned away and sipped at her coffee.

"Rebecca, take the damn pill. You still have some of the medication from yesterday in your bloodstream. When it wears off completely you're gonna be in serious pain." His voice was low, uneasy.

There was no way she was taking it. She didn't like feeling out of control and she disliked being told what to do even less. "No." She glanced at him from the corner of her eye and continued to drink her coffee. He walked back into the kitchen shaking his head.

* * * * *

Several hours later Rebecca woke from her restless sleep to find Jackson sitting on the bed beside her, smoothing her hair back from her face and speaking softly to her. He'd finally talked her into lying down in the bed. It wasn't long till she fell asleep. Now the pain in her head was unbearable. It woke her and brought tears to her eyes. "Baby, please take the Vicodin."

She squinted up at him. His concerned expression made her feel bad for ever fighting him. She rose up on her elbow and took the pill. "I'm sorry, Jackson," she whispered weakly.

He kissed her lightly. "Shh…rest, Becca."

She lay back and closed her eyes again. She didn't feel so tough anymore. She felt the bed sag as Jackson slipped in beside her and gathered her to him. The badass cop part of her gave way to the woman in need. She turned toward him and snuggled closer. He kissed the top of her head and she sighed. For the first time in fifteen years she felt at home.

* * * * *

Rebecca paced the room waiting for Jackson to get out of the shower. Several days had passed since the wreck and she felt much better. Still a little sore and a lot bored and irritated. She wanted to get back to work. Jackson promised just one more day and like a fool she relented and agreed. But now she was going stir crazy.

She heard Jackson turn on the shower. A wicked thought crawled through her mind and she smiled as she walked down the hall and opened the door to the bathroom. Steam billowed out as she stepped in quietly. She could see the silhouette of Jackson's well-defined body through the translucent shower curtain.

Her mouth watered, her nipples tightened, and her cunt spasmed in anticipation. She bit her lip and quietly pushed her pajama pants down and pulled her top over her head. Jackson spun around when she pulled the curtain back. He stood there, water sluicing over the tan muscular planes as his gaze traveled over her naked body. She watched his cock respond immediately and she couldn't help but smile.

Stepping into the tub, she ran her hands over his shoulders, down his chest as the steaming water flowed over them both. Jackson grasped her hips and pulled her close. His mouth slid over hers with lips made slick by the water and she sipped at him as he teased her with slow strokes of his tongue.

She moaned, pressing tighter against him as his hands slid over her ass, gently massaging her. His fingers delved deeper, sliding through the slick honey collecting between the swelling sensitive lips of her pussy. His cock hardened, thickened as it probed her lower abdomen. He pulled away, his breath labored. "Becca...God, baby, I don't want to hurt you."

"You won't." She kissed his jaw, his neck, his shoulder. She nibbled and licked and sucked at his skin. He bent his head and took her nipple into his mouth, sucking, his tongue stroking, sending spirals of desire curling through her, drawing throaty moans from her as tiny ripples sent her vagina into micro spasms of pleasure. She sifted her fingers through his hair and pulled him closer. "I've missed your plump, sweet berries, Becca," he murmured against her skin.

Her hand wrapped around his cock, stroking him slowly. He groaned, his mouth devouring hers. He cupped her breasts, lathering them, his fingers skillfully plucking her aching nipples. She trembled in his arms. Was that ringing in her head?

Jackson cursed colorfully. "I'm sorry, baby, I gotta get the phone." He kissed her hard and stepped out of the shower quickly.

"Well, hell." Her body hummed, ached—no, screamed—for completion. She sighed shakily and washed her body and her hair hurriedly. Turning off the shower she got out. No sense in wasting water. She grabbed a towel and wrapped it around her body. Opening the tiny closet she grabbed another for her hair.

She walked down the hall. Jackson was still on the phone, holding a towel around his waist. Might as well put on the coffee. She ran her fingertips over his flat stomach as she passed him, not missing the way the towel tented just a little lower.

"No, Bryan, you did the right thing. I'm glad you called me about it." Jackson winked at her but she could tell something was troubling him. She leaned back against the counter and watched him.

"Right." He nodded, his frown deepening. "Well, rude is normal for them. Tell me exactly what they asked."

She wished she could hear the other side of the conversation. It was driving her nuts watching Jackson clench his teeth, that muscle in his jaw jump.

"Uh huh. Yeah, that was odd. Don't worry about it, Bryan. I need you to get better as soon as you can. What's the doc say?" He paused, shifting from one leg to the other. "Good, good. I'll come see you soon."

He looked up at her and his expression softened. "She's good." He chuckled and Rebecca frowned. "Exactly. Okay, you bet. If you need anything, call. Don't hesitate. Bye."

"What was that all about?" Rebecca asked, watching Jackson closely. He stalked toward her. Bracing his hands on the counter on either side of her he leaned down and sucked at her neck. Her eyes drifted closed as she tilted her head to give him better access. "Bryan." He lifted her, setting her on the counter and kissed the top swells of her breasts. "Martin and Roby...were asking him...some questions...they shouldn't care about... I have to go deal with this, Becca."

"Okay, I'll go get dressed," she said, jumping down.

Jackson laid his hands on her shoulders. "No, you promised. You aren't one hundred percent yet. I'll feel better if you stay here."

"Well I won't. I'm fine, Jackson..." she argued.

"You promised." He held up one finger.

"You don't play fair," Rebecca scowled.

Jackson leaned down and kissed her. "When I get back, we'll pick up where we left off."

"Hrumph." Rebecca muttered, going to the fridge. "You got any cucumbers in here?"

Chapter Nineteen

Rebecca sat on the edge of the couch with the remote in her hand flipping channels without really paying attention to what she saw. There was nothing on anyway. Just soaps and Springer, neither of which Rebecca wanted to waste her time on. As if she didn't have all kinds of time to waste. She clicked off the television and set the remote on the coffee table, sighing heavily, strumming her fingers on her knee.

What was Jackson doing? Had he found the camper? The waiting, the inactivity, made her feel useless, which made her irritable. The memory of the baby's cry gnawed at her. She was well enough to do some investigating of her own. Why in the hell did she give Jackson one more day? Why did she make that promise? If he had a home computer she could at least check some things out on that. She took a deep breath and blew it out.

She had to find something to occupy her mind or she'd lose it. It hadn't taken long to dress in her denim shorts and one of Jackson's blue cotton T-shirts. She tied the long hem in a knot at her hip. Rebecca had taken her time braiding her hair and dressing, but that hadn't taken long either. She almost wished Jackson was a slob. As much as she hated cleaning up, it would at least give her something to do.

She was sick to death of puttering around the apartment. She stood and wandered into the kitchen to refill her coffee mug then crossed to the sliding glass doors in the dining area. She pulled back the drapes, such a beautifully sunny day. Jackson had a pretty decent little balcony. A small table and chaise sat to one side. Perfect for lounging with a good book.

Reading would pass the time until Jackson got back and she could find out what in the hell was going on. She went to the entertainment center and scanned Jackson's small collection of books. Tom Clancy, figures; Stephen King, a definite maybe. She curled her lip at the one Louis L'Amour. Oh well, it wasn't like she expected he'd have J.D. Robb or Linda Howard. She continued browsing and lifted a brow when she came across *The Complete Works of William Shakespeare*. Poor Bill, he thought he knew so much about women. She smiled and shook her head.

She selected a Stephen King novel and tucked it under her arm as she grabbed the cordless phone. With some effort she got the sliding glass doors unlocked and the security bar removed and stepped out into the warm humid Tennessee June, closing the door behind her. She gazed around at the wooded hillside and marveled at the beautiful view. She breathed in the honeysuckle-scented air. It was such a great change from the city. Setting the mug on the little table she dropped her book.

"Crap." She set the phone down and bent to pick up the novel when she heard a pop and the glass door behind her shattered. Rebecca jerked her head around without lifting it and caught the glimmer of sunlight on metal. Her training kicked in, the cop in her took over. She gritted her teeth and snatched the phone from the table. Another shot hit the brick wall inches from her head.

Adrenaline flooded her blood stream as she picked away shards of glass and pried the door open. She stayed as low as she could as she quickly crawled back into the apartment. It wasn't until she was in the hallway that she stood and ran to the bedroom. She grabbed her gun belt off the hook inside the closet door, un-holstered it and ran back to see if she could catch sight of the shooter.

She crouched low and held the gun steady. With one hand she pressed the buttons to call Jackson's cell phone. She figured the shooter had already gone, if he was smart he would be. She scanned the tree line for signs of movement anyway.

"Answer, dammit," she hissed impatiently.

"Yeah," Jackson answered tersely.

"Jackson, you need to come home." Rebecca kept her voice even.

"Becca, what is it? What's wrong?" Jackson's deep voice took on an uneasy edge.

"A sniper took out your sliding glass door." Her reply was low-pitched and deceptively dispassionate.

"Fuck!" Jackson growled and disconnected.

Rebecca dropped the phone and used both hands to aim her gun. Assholes, evidently they wanted to finish the job. Well, fuck them. They'd underestimated her. She moved to the edge of the doors and pulled the curtains aside. Her gaze shifted from the woods to the surrounding area. Her eyes sharp, she focused on taking steady breaths, keeping her cool. She struggled to rein in her fury.

She doubted the sniper would try to enter the apartment, he was probably long gone by now. She snarled, hoping he did try to come for her. She'd take his sorry ass out, maybe take out both kneecaps and torture him till he told her who had that baby. Her mind went back to the child she'd failed to help. Did they still have him? Was he safe? Fuck! She had to do something. To hell with this convalescent shit. It wasn't like her but she would have to break that promise. She had wasted too much time lying around. The bastards were still shooting at her and that just pissed her off.

It had only been minutes when she heard the echo of footfalls on the stairwell outside the door. She moved to the hallway and trained her revolver on the door with perfect aim, as the deadbolts were swiftly unlocked.

Jackson burst through the door with his gun raised and his teeth set. He met Rebecca's gaze and advanced on her as he holstered his weapon. "Aw hell, Becca," he bit out, his eyes cold and dark.

Rebecca lowered her gun with a sigh. "We need to check out back."

"You're bleeding," he snapped.

She looked down at the blood that flowed down her shins and shrugged. She hadn't felt anything. They were probably just nicks. Before she could take a step toward the door, Jackson scooped her up and carried her into the bathroom. She fought him but he held her firmly.

"Be still. Did you get a shot at him?"

"No, he was gone by the time I retrieved my weapon. Damn it to hell, Jackson, this is ridiculous." He sat her on the closed lid of the toilet and knelt in front of her. "We need to canvas the woods out back. He was in the woods. Are you listening to me!?" she asked, trying to slap his hands away.

He wet a washcloth in the sink beside them and wrung it out. "Sandor Kylie and Gray Jensen are taking care of it, now shut up," he replied sharply without looking at her.

"Shut up? Shut up?" she yelled, eyeing him incredulously, ignoring the sting as he carefully washed away the blood. "Who the hell are Sandor Kylie and Gray Jensen?"

"State Troopers. They're working with me, us. You may need stitches..." he said. His voice shook with rage.

"Too fuckin' bad," she hissed. "I'm not going back to the hospital. I'm sick of you babying me. I'm not fragile, Jack..."

Jackson took her face between her hands and kissed her hard, fast, silencing her tirade. It wasn't tender, it was a kiss that meant to stake claim. When he pulled away she was panting. Her lips felt swollen and bruised. It pissed her off even more that her body so readily responded to him. His expression had her swallowing her biting retort. She shuddered at the warning, the fury and the fear she saw in his eyes.

His thumb caressed her jaw; his gaze searched her face. Her heart pounded against her ribs. Again his mouth closed over hers. His lips moved with aching gentleness, sending ripples of need curling through her.

"We found the casings, Jackson, but he cleared out...oh sorry." Gray stood at the bathroom door, Sandor stood behind him.

Jackson pulled away with a growl. Rebecca blinked and sucked in air. She looked up at the bathroom doorway. Both men looked as uncomfortable as Rebecca felt.

"I figured as much," Jackson said tightly.

"You all right?" Sandor asked Rebecca, lifting his brows. He had a hard face and sad eyes. He watched her closely, his brow lifted as he waited for her answer.

"Yes, I'm fine," she muttered. Jackson was shaken. She could plainly see that, felt it in his kiss.

"I'm taking her to the emergency room. I'll meet you guys back at the station."

Oh that was it, the last straw. Now she was embarrassed as well as aroused, frustrated and angry. She really wanted to punch something. She glanced back at Jackson, her hard gaze matching his. She could almost hear the crackle of tension between them. "The hell I am," she said through her teeth.

"Stubborn woman," he growled at her. "You may need a tetanus shot."

She glared at him. "Had one, two years ago. I'm current. Just give me a fuckin' band-aid."

"It doesn't look so bad, Jackson." Gray stepped into the cramped space. He stood over them, his hands on his hips. His bulky frame clad in a beige uniform, gun at his hip. Damn, he made that ugly uniform look good. Rebecca felt suffocated. Too many big, controlling men in too small a space. Gray's eyes were hard as he examined her wound, tilting his head. "Put some antibiotic ointment on it. She'll be fine."

Chapter Twenty

Give her a fuckin' band-aid. Jackson snorted as he slapped one in her palm, and then jerked the antibiotic ointment from the medicine cabinet and gave it to her as well. He wanted to snarl at Sandor and Gray, but he wasn't afforded that option at the moment.

Both men were too damned close to her to suit him anyway. As though her ankles, or the long, pretty expanse of leg they kept glancing at was any of their business.

He glanced back at the two men, frowning fiercely. He didn't like the gleam of amusement that came to their eyes.

"We're leaving the apartment," he told her as the other two men finally filed out of the cramped area. "We're in deep shit here, Becca. Get dressed and re-pack that bag while I get things together with Sandor and Gray."

"What kind of deep shit? Did you find out something about that baby?" Her voice was filled with excitement now.

Jackson wiped his hands over his face. She would be the death of him. She slapped the band-aid on her shin and followed him quickly as he left the room. He glanced back at her, seeing the glitter in her eyes, the flush on her cheeks and the intent, determined expression on her face. Hell. He wanted to fuck her, not take her out into a damned war.

"We found something out, but I don't know where the child is involved yet," he growled as they entered the bedroom.

He slammed the door shut behind him. His cock was raging, but he'd be damned if he'd let Sandor and Gray hear the helpless little cries of pleasure that came from his Becca's throat as he made love to her.

"What did you find out?" She jerked her suitcase out of the closet ahead of him and tossed it on the bed.

Glancing back at him curiously, she moved to the dresser for her clothes.

"Save a pair of jeans to wear out of here," he told her, crossing his arms over his chest as he watched her. She was raring to go, dammit. He had hoped to talk her into staying someplace nice and safe while he, Sandor and Gray moved in to find out what the hell the mayor and his henchmen were up to.

She nodded quickly. "Now tell me what's going on."

He sighed wearily. "We're not completely certain, Becca. But it looks like someone is using Jericho to hide Middle Eastern illegals. We think it could be the families of certain terrorist factions."

Becca stopped packing. He watched her face.

"What?" He narrowed his eyes, seeing a sudden dawning realization in her eyes.

"When I was on the force in Detroit, there was an investigation. I suspected someone on the force of aiding Middle Eastern terrorists in slipping their families across the border into Canada. Nothing came of it, but…"

"Todd's here, causing trouble." Jackson clenched his fists as he tucked them into his pants pockets. "Was he part of the investigation?"

Becca licked her lips nervously. "It was rumored he was under investigation, not part of the investigation," she whispered. "Nothing came of it, though." She shook her head desperately. "It was just a rumor."

Jackson shook his head. "In this case, I'd suspect it was no mere rumor," he sighed. "Sandor and Gray were investigating on this end. They're part of a national taskforce, and Todd Lawrence's name pops up in more than one memo concerning problems Detroit is having tracking this situation. When he showed up here, he raised more than a little interest."

Her eyes lit with an angry gleam. "That's treason," she said quietly.

Jackson was silent for a moment before he sighed wearily. "Yes, Becca, that's treason. Which makes Todd incredibly stupid and dangerous. We suspect the mayor as well as Roby and Martin of conspiring with them. Now get ready, get packed. I have to talk to Sandor and Gray, and see how we're going to do this."

He walked to her, hating the hurt in her eyes. She looked disillusioned, betrayed.

"I thought he was just an asshole, not a traitor," she whispered. "Will they suspect me now? Of helping him?"

They had, Jackson knew. Sandor had been very blunt in giving that information. Until the incident with the truck. The description Becca had given of the driver matched with a suspected arms dealer involved in the transportation of the terrorist families. Her injuries, her attempts to stop the truck, and now the attempt on her life pretty much cleared her of suspicion.

"No, Becca," he promised, pulling her into his arms as he kissed her forehead gently. "No one suspects you, baby. But you are in danger now. You can identify the driver, and you know the dangers involved in that. We have to take care of this before you'll be safe. Now get ready."

He pulled back, but he couldn't resist lowering his head to kiss her trembling lips. His hunger for her was unlike anything he had ever known. He craved the taste of her…yeah, that soft trembling moan. His body tightened, his cock raging instantly in demand.

Her mouth opened for him, her tongue tangling with his timidly as her hands gripped his shoulders. She wasn't timid for long though. Jackson groaned as she moved against him, her hands moving to his hair, her lips opening farther, her mouth becoming hungry now as the kiss intensified. Kissing her was like feeding fire, and it was threatening to rage out of control.

He tightened his grip on his control, easing back shakily as she moaned at the desertion.

"Damn, baby," he sighed, laying his forehead against hers as he stared down at her. "You burn me alive."

He touched her cheek gently before releasing her. Her skin was soft, though still pale. But the pain was gone from her eyes. They were slumberous now, and rich with passion. That look made him want to eat her live.

She drew a deep breath, causing her hard tipped breasts to push against the fabric of his shirt. Damn. He wanted to rip the shirt from her and immerse himself in the heat and fiery passion that belonged to Becca alone.

"Jackson…" He saw the emotion in her eyes, the words trembling on her lips and waited breathlessly. "Nothing." Disappointment raged through him as she shook her head and moved carefully away from him.

"Sure?" Damn her, she was stubborn. Or was he merely indulging in more wishful thinking than the situation deserved?

He loved her. There was no damned doubt about it. He had loved her when she was a kid, loved her when she was sixteen, and he was so damned crazy about her now he could hardly see straight for it.

"Yeah." She cleared her throat, moving back to her suitcase. "Do whatever you need to do. I'll be ready in less than thirty minutes."

Jackson sighed. "Okay, baby. I'll finish out things with Sandor and Gray. We'll be waiting on you in the living room."

He left the room, his cock hard and ready, his heart and mind whirling in confusion. Dammit to hell, she had to love him, why was she being so hesitant? He shook his head, promising himself he would find out soon. As soon as he had her safe.

* * * * *

God help her, she'd almost ruined everything. Rebecca wanted to tell Jackson she loved him. She always had. She always would. There had been something in those eyes of his. Something mesmerizing and powerful. For a moment she thought he might...but she couldn't let herself believe that. She'd made a fool of herself over Jackson Montgomery too many times. She wouldn't do it again.

Her heart was still pounding, her nipples ached, sending pulses of need radiating through her. She closed her eyes and bit her lip. Her pussy throbbed and every step caused a silken sliding friction that made her want to plead for release. With her love came this all-consuming lust, hunger, desire. Whatever the hell it was, it wasn't like anything she'd ever known and it wasn't something she could ignore.

She pulled off her shorts and with a grimace, her underwear. She was gonna need panty liners with Jackson around all the time. Quickly she found some clean panties and pulled them on, followed by her jeans. She stuffed her dirty clothes into the back pocket of her suitcase and then zipped it close and set it beside the bedroom door.

Todd certainly hadn't made her yearn like this. Todd... What in God's name had she seen in him? She'd thought maybe she loved him once. She had admired his strength, his intelligence, his independence. He had never demanded of her time, he had his thing and she had hers. She sighed and sat on the edge of the bed and dug through her purse for a ponytail holder.

At the time, it seemed the perfect relationship until the abuse started. Rebecca shuddered at the memory of his tirades, the threats and accusations, the name-calling, deriding her in front of fellow officers. It had been too much so she broke it off, or tried to. She swallowed the knot lodged in her throat, clenched her teeth, ran her shaking hands through her hair vigorously and fastened it loosely with the blue scrunchie she found. All this time he was a traitor. A fucking traitor!

And now he was trying to use her. Had she been used before? It made her skin crawl to think about it. She wanted the weasel to feel pain. Lots of pain, hideous, gruesome, tremendous pain. And she wanted it to be at her hand. Although she was pretty sure if Jackson got to him first there would be very little left of him to hurt. Well, she thought as she stood, she'd just have to get to Officer Lawrence first now, wouldn't she?

Chapter Twenty-One

Jackson stood with his back to her, his hands on his hips, talking to the state cops. Damn…his ass looked so good, she wanted to bite it. Rebecca gave herself a mental head slap. It didn't matter what was going on, just the sight of him turned her into an inferno. Her insides melted, her vagina clenched. She nearly moaned out loud. Damn. Sandor and Gray didn't look bad either.

"We intercepted a transmission reporting another delivery," Sandor said. His voice was a commanding deep bass.

"From where was it sent?" Jackson asked.

"Morocco," Sandor answered.

"Let me guess, the report was meant for Lawrence."

Gray nodded. "They're moving major players in the terrorist ring this time."

Sandor glanced briefly at Gray then fixed his gaze on Jackson again. "We're not sure if there will be family involved with this one or not but we know there's a family in Jericho now that will be moving on. We're expecting activities within the next day or two. Just lay low and watch. If you observe anything, report it immediately."

Jackson's back stiffened. Rebecca would be willing to bet his gray eyes were narrowed.

Gray sighed, reading Jackson's body language. "Look, I completely understand how you must feel, but if you go 'Rambo' out there you'll blow the whole thing."

"I'm not a 'stand by and watch' kind of guy but I'm not wet behind the ears and I'm not an idiot, either. I'll do what needs to be done," Jackson bit out.

"Good." Sandor's frown deepened. Did the man never smile? "We'll be heading to Nashville today to coordinate with the taskforce being prepped there."

Rebecca cleared her throat and their gazes shifted past Jackson to focus on her. With their closed expressions, broad chests, and massive biceps they were an intimidating sight to behold. Even without the wide shiny black gun belt hanging low on their narrow hips. She suddenly felt sorry for anyone who tangled with these boys.

Sandor stood just a little taller than Gray, his black hair was wavy and a bit mussed from the wide brimmed olive hat he held in his hand. Those vivid green eyes of his were revealing. There was a story there. The corner of Gray's mouth lifted a bit and the half smile made his blue eyes sparkle. Did he just wink? She could have been mistaken. Maybe he had a twitch. Jackson turned and frowned at her. What had she done now? Sheesh.

"Ready?" Jackson's tone was a bit strained. He took her suitcase and pulled her firmly to his side as she walked up and stood beside him.

Rebecca lifted her chin and narrowed her eyes. "Yes."

"Good." He grunted and nodded to the troopers who turned and walked out ahead of them.

* * * * *

The back seat of a patrol car was not designed for comfort. Rebecca shifted, trying to relieve the cramp in her thigh. "Will someone fill me in now?" she snapped. She met Sandor's gaze in the rear view mirror and when he didn't say anything she lifted her brows and he looked back at the road. She turned to Jackson sitting beside her. His long legs made him decidedly more uncomfortable than she was.

"We believe they're using the rest stop off the interstate as a pick up and drop off point. There's a network of caves right above it. You and I are going to camp there and stake it out. Sandor and Gray are taking us to pick up another vehicle then we'll take an old back road up to the caves," Jackson said, holding her gaze. "Everything's already set up."

"We expected they'd try to take you out, Officer Taylor," Sandor interrupted. He didn't like explaining himself, she could tell by his tone. "So we had things put in place to send you and Sheriff Montgomery on the stakeout. That way you're safe and you're useful at the same time."

Useful? Ha. He had no idea. She hated being underestimated. "And we will be in communication with those two?" She nodded toward the front seat without taking her gaze from his. She couldn't look away from the storm brewing in his eyes.

"Yes and others working on the case." He lowered his voice a bit. "Are you up for this?"

Rebecca snorted. "I am so up for this." She finally turned away. Her tone did nothing to hide her desire for revenge. She could still feel Jackson watching her. Sandor too. She knew they were concerned. They probably thought she was too emotionally involved. But she didn't care, there was too much at stake here. She never thought of herself as overly patriotic but since September eleventh everyone had become more passionate about America. She was no different. And the fact that she'd been used, was still being used by that little piss ant of a man...it made her livid.

So the baby was part of a family being smuggled out of the Middle East. But he sounded so young, just an infant and that had been a cry of pain. Was he sick or injured? Was he being abused? She jumped when Jackson enveloped her hand in his, linking his fingers with hers.

The warmth of his hand, the caress of his thumb, soothed her building irritation some. She closed her eyes. When had she let her guard down and fallen all the way? God, she loved him more than she thought she was capable of loving anyone. If he didn't love her back, she was really going to be hurt. Real serious pain.

She squeezed his hand, shifted again and frowned out the window. The road began to narrow and the homes became farther apart. They turned off onto a wooded dirt road. It wasn't long until the woods became denser, the road rougher. Finally they came to a stop. Gray got out and opened the door for them. Sandor continued to watch in the rearview mirror.

Rebecca got out of the car and stretched her arms up over her head. Out of the corner she saw Gray's appreciative gaze. Jackson didn't try to hide his scowl as he went to the back of the car and lifted her suitcase from the trunk. She lowered her arms and quickly pulled her shirt down, clearing her throat.

Gray's eyes were bright with humor. Rebecca could tell Gray enjoyed pressing Jackson's buttons with his subtle flirting. "Follow this road about five hundred feet then turn right onto an overgrown path. The jeep will be sitting there. It's loaded with everything you'll need. Follow the path about three miles and you'll see a stick in the ground with a neon orange tie on it. Pull it up and turn there into the wooded area. Around the corner and almost on the edge of the cliff you'll find the mouth of the cave," he said as he got back into the patrol car. "Be sure and watch for it or you'll pass it right up." He smiled at Rebecca and winked. She was sure of it this time. "Be careful. We'll be in touch."

Jackson nodded. "Thanks," he said blandly and began walking.

Gray got back in the car and Rebecca heard them backing up as she jogged to catch up with Jackson. They walked in silence until they came to the jeep. It was painted camouflage green, black and gray; and it was fully loaded. They had night goggles, weapons, two-way radios, a cell phone, food, matches, lanterns…everything they could possibly need was there.

She climbed in next to Jackson. "You okay?" she asked, laying a hand on his forearm.

He looked at her as he turned the ignition. She felt a shiver slide up her spine. A mixture of heat and anger gathered there, then softened. He leaned over and kissed her lightly on the lips. "I'm fine."

She kept quiet for most of the teeth rattling way. She held on tight to the roll bar to keep from being thrown out. Gray was right; the marker was inconspicuous. She hopped out and pulled it up, throwing it in the back then walked around the rest of the way.

The mouth of the cave was secluded, shielded by bushes and undergrowth. Jackson drove the jeep as far into the brush as he could and did his best to secure it.

The mouth of the cave was small, so Jackson had to duck. Rebecca didn't expect there'd be as much space inside as there was. It opened up into a room big enough for all their equipment and a fire if they needed one. Someone had already swept it out and kindling was piled along one wall with a stack of firewood.

"This will be pretty comfortable." Jackson scanned the room then glanced at her. "Let's hurry and unload the jeep."

When they had everything they needed unloaded and stored in the cave, Jackson put the top up on the jeep and it seemed to dissolve into the foliage. Inside the cave, lanterns sent shadows and light dancing over the walls. It was cool, but not cool enough for a fire. The sun was going down and Rebecca was thankful for the bug repellant. She sat cross-legged on her thick bedroll loading her pistol.

"Come here," Jackson said without turning. She pulled herself up and went to where he stood right outside the cave. He put his arm around her. "Look, down there is the rest stop. You see?"

"Yeah, pretty clear view." Even with the dim light she could see the block building through the trees and the people walking back and forth from the building to the various cars, trucks and campers. "Shouldn't be difficult to get what we need," she muttered.

"We have a video camera with infra red." Jackson nodded.

"Cool." Rebecca grinned up at him. "A new toy… I get to use it."

Jackson chuckled and kissed her nose. "We'll see."

She scowled at him. "Oh yeah. You'll see." She looked back down at the rest stop. "What about Todd, will he be showing up here?"

"I don't know." She felt him watching her now. His touch heated her blood, her nipples hardened in response as his hand moved down over her hip and up again, but she tried to ignore it. "Becca."

Conflicting emotions swirled in her stomach as she kept her eyes on the rest stop. Jackson turned to stand in front of her, blocking her view. He lifted her chin and waited till she met his gaze. What she thought she saw in his eyes made her breath hitch.

Before she could say anything his mouth closed over hers, his tongue stroking the tender inside of her lips. Desire bloomed in her womb and spread through her body like a flash fire as he pulled her close, his hands holding her body tightly against his. Her nipples hardened against his chest, his thigh moved between hers and she swallowed his groan. His hands moved over her ass, kneading, lifting her against his hard thigh, then his bulging erection.

"Jackson. We need to be watching," she moaned against his mouth as she threaded her fingers through his hair.

"It's early yet. Nothing will happen for hours," he murmured as he nibbled along her jaw line, her earlobe, her neck. "Baby, I have to taste you, feel you now. I won't get another chance later." Her body was vibrating with need. Liquid heat flooded her sensitive folds; her cunt undulated, waiting to be filled with him. Only him.

Chapter Twenty-Two

Jackson's mouth devoured hers, his head tilted, his tongue licking then delving past her lips, her teeth, to stroke the delicate interior. He sipped at her tongue, nibbled at her lips as he stalked her, pressing her back until she found herself wedged between the rough cool stone and the searing heat of Jackson's solid hard body. The provocative way he moved against her, abrading her swollen nipples through her bra, the soft cotton of her shirt, heightened her arousal.

He leaned away from her body, but only enough to touch her face, to caress the rounded sides of her breasts. They felt as though they were swelling, filling his big hands with her heated flesh. His thumbs massaged her nipples. She squirmed as his hand moved lower, slowly, as though he loved the feel of her stomach, her navel, flooding her senses with every erotic touch. He unbuttoned her jeans. His fingers trailed lower, just above the elastic band of her panties. Gently, lightly, he teased the ultra sensitive skin and she felt she was going up in flames.

His hand slid inside her panties to the curls covering her mound, and over the pouting lips of her sex. His fingers moved over the crevice between, drawing her juices over her swelling flesh. His mouth muted her cries as his fingers probed between her slick folds. She ground her hips against his hand as his tongue moved inside her mouth, mimicking the way his fingers stroked her saturated pussy.

Her breath was coming in pants as she clutched at his shoulders. She wrapped a leg around his hip and pulled him closer as she pushed her pelvis against the straining bulge of his cock. A sound that was greedy and raw escaped his throat and his hands became rough and hungry.

With his free hand he shoved her shirt and bra up together, freeing her breasts. He growled, taking one taut peak inside his hot mouth. His tongue flicked over it and she grit her teeth and swallowed her scream. His finger plunged inside her, stroking her as the juices flowing from her gripping flesh flooded his hand. Her mind was fuzzy, her whole focus on the building tension growing, throbbing within her. She cried out, unable to stop herself. He was taking her to the edge and she was helpless.

"Shhh, baby," he whispered hoarsely against her throbbing lips.

"I can't," she whimpered, licking her swollen lips, and tore at his shirt. She wasn't sure how she got his shirt off and she didn't care. She loved this man; she wanted this man, like she'd never wanted anyone. She was voracious. Her need, her desire was like a hot current running along every nerve.

She pulled him closer, loving the feel of his warm smooth skin, the ripple of his muscles as he pleasured her. Her nails bit into his hard bulging biceps. She licked and bit and sucked his neck. Her blood was raging through her veins, demanding more of him. She needed to feel him inside her.

Her hands slid down his chest, unfastened his jeans and freed him. His hot, rock-hard cock filled her hand and she stroked him. She kissed him, sucked his bottom lip. Her thumb smoothed over his velvety tip, the drop of pre-cum spreading as she explored. She stroked down his shaft, feeling the blood pulse rapidly through the bulging veins as he jerked against her. "Fuck me, Jackson," she whimpered breathlessly in his ear.

He yanked the shirt and bra over her head and threw it aside. She opened her eyes and met his dark gaze. "God, you're making me crazy," he snarled low before possessing her mouth again. She cried into his mouth as he shoved her pants down.

Her world tilted and she found herself lying on the bedroll. He held her effortlessly, as though she were weightless. He pulled her jeans off with a single tug. She lay there, overheated, naked, watching him as he stepped out of his own jeans and knelt between her legs. His strength and the power of his lust for her had her trembling in anticipation.

He grasped her hips and pulled her forward, and she rose up, straddling him as she wrapped her arms around his neck. His cock nestled between the sopping engorged lips of her cunt and she gasped. His hands caressed her ass, slowly moving her back and forth, letting the round swollen head glide against her throbbing clit.

Rebecca kissed him frantically, moaning into his mouth. He groaned and cupped her breast, weighing and kneading it as his mouth moved down, nibbling her collarbone, his tongue laving her other breast. She arched her back as his teeth grazed her nipple, sending her spiraling out of control. She clutched at him, panting as her head fell back.

His hand fisted in her hair and he pulled her to him. His mouth covered hers swallowing her screams as her orgasm seized her. It pounded through her and her body shuddered from the force of it. Jackson didn't give her time to recover. He lifted her then, impaling her onto his thick shaft; he filled her, her rippling flesh clutching at his invading cock. She clung to him as the waves crashed over her again and again.

"So tight," he groaned as he began to move inside her. "So hot, wet, tight."

She pressed against him and rode. Her body, coated with sweat, slid against him. Every brush of her erect nipples against his chest sent spirals of pleasure surging through her, coiling tighter and tighter, building. "Harder, Jackson," she croaked.

"Yeah, baby. Wrap your legs around me." He held her hips still while she leaned back bracing her body on her arms, her hands fisted in the padded bedroll. "Tighter, hold on tighter." She tried to catch her breath as she did as he instructed, locking her ankles behind his back.

Jackson supported her shoulders, neck and head with one arm. The other supported her back as he slammed into her. Hard. Every thrust sent mind-numbing pleasure thundering through her. The sound of their labored breathing, the slapping of wet flesh against wet flesh, intensified her need.

She clenched her thighs around him, arching, thrusting upward, taking him in, all of him. She heard the small cries that came from her, they sounded far away. She tightened the walls of her sheath around him, feeling the friction as he withdrew and drove into her again. She was focused only on Jackson, the pleasure that engulfed her, the pleasure that she was giving him.

Her climax shattered into a million tiny shards of sensation. She rose up clutching at his arms, her breath caught in her throat and she struggled not to scream. She bit her lip as low strangled moans escaped from deep inside. Jackson plunged deeper and deeper, touching her womb. Rebecca couldn't distinguish between the pain and the pleasure.

Her cunt spasmed again and again, her slick cream flowing from her with every climax, coating his pistoning shaft, his balls as they slapped against her. The ripples of ecstasy she thought were fading swelled and grew and tore through her again. She thought she might die and she didn't give a damn. Her heart pounded, her body flooded with overwhelming sensation.

Jackson bared his teeth as he surged inside her again, then once more. His gaze locked with hers. He groaned, his hot cum filling her. Her pulsing cunt captured him, milking him.

He lifted her body and held her close. "My Becca," he murmured as he changed positions and laid back, her body draping over him, his semi-rigid cock still inside her. She closed her eyes, nuzzling his chest. She felt sated, limp, and so in love, shuddering as aftershocks vibrated through her. If he only knew how much hope she put in those two words.

For a moment she lay still, giving her body time to cool, her breathing to even out. Jackson ran a hand over her hair and kissed her forehead. It was such a tender thing to do, so intimate. She knew he cared, and for now that was enough. She kissed his chest; her tongue caressed his flat brown nipple. She smiled at his sharp intake of breath, felt the pulses of blood pumping into his shaft, making him swell and lengthen inside her again.

He closed his eye on a groan and lifted his hips, pushing himself deeper. Slowly she rose over him, her hands splayed on his chest, bracing herself above him. He opened his eyes and met her gaze. She moved slowly, pulling away and taking him in again. She flexed the muscled walls of her vagina as she sheathed him and his lids lowered over stormy gray eyes.

His hands gripped her hips. Hard, rigid muscle rippled under her fingers as they circled his nipples and skimmed over his sweat-dampened body. "You feel so good." She moaned, riding him with achingly slow strokes, his cock like steel, stretching, filling her. His hands cupped her heaving breasts, his thumbs grazing her stiff aching nipples. She groaned as she picked up the pace, her juices gathered and flowed from her.

His hand moved down her stomach and glided through the wet thatch of curls to the top of her pussy. He found her clit and rubbed, circled it, as she rotated her hips, grinding against him. She whimpered as his cock pressed against her G-spot. Her head fell forward, letting her long hair trail over his chest.

"Mmm, feels good, Becca. Yeah, baby, do that. Oh yeah." He grasped her hips again, his fingers biting into her flesh as he arched his hips to meet her circling thrusts.

She spread her legs wider and arched her back, bouncing harder and faster. She couldn't contain the small breathy cries that came from deep inside her as long violent waves of sensation crashed over her. Her body trembled, bathed in a gripping euphoria. She bit her lip to keep from screaming out her release.

She watched the passion swirl in Jackson's eyes. She was mesmerized by his expression. His hooded gaze held hers as he growled, baring his teeth. He didn't give her climax time to decrease in intensity before he took control and changed positions with her, carefully turning her onto her stomach without leaving her body.

His knees were between hers, pressing her thighs farther apart. His arm banded around her stomach as he surged into her with deep soul-shaking thrusts that had her screaming into the pillow. She cried out with every explosion of pleasure as climax after climax ripped through her, every time his balls slapped against her clit, every time he slammed into her. Her body was raging with incredible and frenzied sensations. He groaned her name as he erupted, filling her with hot cream, soothing her.

Exhausted, they collapsed together; he lay on his side pulling her against him, sweeping the damp curls away from her face and neck. He kissed her cheek, her neck. "You're so soft, baby, so sweet." He nibbled and licked at the tender skin behind her ear. "I'll never get enough of you. The way you feel, the way you taste." Her stomach quivered as his hand splayed over her soft skin. "But, I'll let you have a few minutes to recuperate."

Rebecca breathed deeply and turned in his arms. She smiled and touched his face. "Thanks, I've never felt so good for so long. I'm not sure it was good for my system. I'm afraid I'll need more than a few minutes to come back down to earth."

His lips curved as he bent to kiss her gently at first then more deeply. His tongue rubbed against hers sensuously.

"Or, maybe not," she moaned, pressing against him. Her body responded to his so readily. Even though she still shook with aftershocks, her clit aching, her vagina throbbing from over stimulation, with only a kiss he could still seduce her. She still wanted him; she'd never stop wanting him.

Chapter Twenty-Three

It was like she stepped into a fantasy world. Fireflies twinkled everywhere like fairy lights. The soft sultry breeze carried the scent of honeysuckle and pine. The melodic sound of the gentle mountain stream as it flowed down over the slick rocks was soothing. Jackson stood waist deep in the deeper part of the water watching her from under lowered lids, a roguish grin curving those wonderfully firm lips. Shadows made him look mysterious, dangerous, exotic, like a mystic king enticing an innocent virgin to sacrifice her purity to please him.

Standing naked on the bank of the creek, her arms wrapped around her stomach, Rebecca shuddered at the thought, and then smirked. She was the farthest thing from virginal but she wasn't immune to his seduction. He was too damn enticing to resist. He quickly sank into the swirling water and emerged again with a splash, smoothing his hair back, the water sluicing off the hard planes of his body.

He caught her gaze again. "You look incredible standing there like that." His voice lowered to a growl. "An incredibly sexy little pixie."

Rebecca grinned. "Pest, Pixie *Pest*. Remember?"

He shook his head slowly. "No, just a whole lotta heat in a tight little package. Mmm, so hot. C'mere, I need to touch you."

"Again?" she teased.

He eyed her a moment and began walking out of the creek toward her. "And again, and again…"

Rebecca watched Jackson's muscles bunch and ripple as he moved toward her and her mouth went dry. His shaft, heavy, jutting, glistened in the waning light. She should back up, she told herself. But her gaze was locked with his and something held her in place. Her body swayed with the impact of his desire for her. Even in the dusky light she could see it there, plain in his eyes.

He took her hand and helped her step down into the stream. He led her to several large smooth stones. The brisk clear water rushed over them faster there and didn't rise much over her ankle.

He lowered himself onto a wide flat stone, careful not to slip. "Here, sit here," he said spreading her legs, his shaft bobbing against the current.

"Sit?" she asked, wide-eyed with a crooked smile.

"Yes, Becca, turn around and sit. The cool water flowing over your tender pussy will feel good.

Rebecca lifted her brows and shrugged. She really was tender but she was still overheated, her flesh still slick and tingling, her nipples erect and aching. She turned and his hands circled her waist, holding her, as she eased herself between his legs. He pulled her back against his chest and pushed her knees apart. The water was just cool enough, flowing gently over her swollen folds, her throbbing clit, washing away her soreness, but did nothing to alleviate the heat of arousal.

"Oh, yeah. This does feel nice." She moaned, spreading her knees farther apart.

Jackson cupped the cool water into his hands and let it spill over her chest, over her breasts. Her nipples contracted into hard tips. His hands covered them, warming them as he massaged her. His substantial manhood pulsed against the small of her back. She leaned her head back on his shoulder and pulled his head down. She licked his full lower lip and his tongue darted out to meet hers. She sighed as she sucked it gently, her lips pressing against his. His hands plucked at her nipples, electrifying her senses. Her blood pounded in her ears.

"We've got to get back, Jackson," she whispered hoarsely.

He sighed deeply and kissed her neck. "I hate it that you're right." He arched his hips against her. "I want to fuck you all night." His voice was raw with mounting hunger.

Rebecca stood and looked down at him. He'd make a great Playgirl centerfold, she thought. He watched her as she gingerly stepped over the rocks to where the water was a bit deeper to rinse the dry, salty sweat from her skin. She turned to see Jackson standing on the bank leaning against a wide oak with his legs crossed, watching her. Rebecca's lips curved into a smile as she stepped onto the bank and stood in front of him. His eyes were turbulent, his body was tense, his cock was raging.

"You ready to go back?" he asked, rubbing a hand up and down her arm, chasing away the goose bumps.

"Not yet," she murmured. His brow furrowed as he searched her face. Taking his face in her hands she touched her lips to his, lingering moments before she moved down his body.

He held his breath and uncrossed his legs. "Becca." He groaned as her tongue circled his navel and trailed lower. She knelt in front of him and grasped his thick erection with both hands. She gazed up at him as she sipped at the broad tip, and licked away the pearl that welled there. Her lips opened over the bulging head, gliding it into her mouth. She ran her tongue along the crease underneath and sucked gently, her finger moved lightly over his shaft. He grasped her head, his fingers weaving through her hair. "Oh God, yes, baby. Take me," he croaked as she sucked him in.

Her lips drew him in, her tongue stroked the pulsing underside of his steely staff. She moaned, loving the taste of him, the sound of his ragged breathing as he urged her to suck him harder. She felt the slick juices gather in the folds of her cunt as she drew on him. One hand closed over the base of his cock, the other cupped his balls and she cautiously massaged the delicate flesh.

She withdrew and sucked him in again. He grunted, pulling her closer, sinking deeper into her mouth. She felt the hot throbbing head of his cock against the back of her throat and swallowed, taking him as deeply as she could. "Suck harder, baby," he growled. "Ah Becca, my Becca."

She felt his balls tighten, his body go rigid, as he thrust into her mouth. Her tongue stroked, her mouth pulled on him longer and harder. He threw his head back with a strangled cry as his seed shot into her mouth in long hot bursts. She swallowed him, taking all he had to give, licked him clean. She looked up at him and smiled, licking the last of him from her lips.

He pulled her off her knees and pulled her into his arms. "You're so damn good, Becca," he murmured, his breathing still labored. His mouth covered hers, melting her bones, curling her toes. Reluctantly, he pulled away, buried his face in her hair and nuzzled her neck.

She held him tight, never wanting to leave that spot, but they had to. Night had fallen and she needed to focus on the job ahead of them now and not on Jackson's hands, or his mouth or his cock…dammit. Carefully, they made their way back to the cave in the dark. If she was going to keep her mind on her work she was going to have to keep him at arm's length.

They decided to watch the rest stop in shifts. Rebecca took the first while Jackson slept close by. He woke up around three and took over while she slept. She slept pretty well, considering. She grinned thinking it was probably the work out that helped. She woke around eight and yawned. "Hey, see anything?" she asked, stretching.

Jackson looked over at her and winked. "Mornin', gorgeous. No, not yet. Got a call from Sandor, though."

"I didn't hear the phone," she said pulling on a clean pair of socks and hiking boots.

Jackson lifted the binoculars and turned his attention back to the rest stop. "It's on vibrate."

"Ah," she said. "So?"

"So, he said they expected activity today. Possibly this afternoon." His expression turned serious.

"Good. Do you think I have time to walk back down to the creek?" she asked. "Girl stuff," she added when he gave her a questioning glance.

Jackson thought a minute. "Okay, but don't take long, and take your gun."

"All right." She strapped her pistol to her hip and headed out.

The rough path that led around the foot of a mountain to the stream looked a bit different in the light of day, Rebecca thought. When the path widened and the cover of trees thinned out, she veered off to the side of the path, careful to stay in the shadows.

She had just reached the clearing when the rumble of a chopper overhead alerted her and had her ducking for cover. She glanced up to see it pass over and hover just as an arm grabbed her around the waist and yanked her farther into the undergrowth, under a thick bush.

"Stay down, Becca." Jackson's voice was a hiss in her ear.

"I'm down," she hissed back. "Why did you follow me?"

"I didn't follow you. I was trained for Special Forces, Becca. I can hear an approaching chopper long before I actually see it." His voice was tight.

"Well, you're just eaten up with talent, aren't you?" Rebecca sniped.

He lifted a brow. "You would know."

She narrowed her eyes and chose to ignore his remark. "It was heading that way." She stood, pointing toward the mountain peak as she brushed the twigs and pine needles from her knees. "Don't you think they've landed somewhere up on the mountain?"

He nodded, listening intently and watching her. "Let's go."

Chapter Twenty-Four

There were few things in the world as beautiful to Jackson as the Tennessee mountains, especially those in Claiborne county. The tall rolling hills, boulder-strewn valleys and steep cliffs had always fascinated him. The sense of history and continuity kept him grounded, reminded him daily why he had joined the Marines, why he had fought in the Middle East, why he had taken the post as sheriff in the small town.

Because some things were just worth fighting for. His uncle's murder had shaken his world, had left him questioning values and beliefs that had sustained him all his life. He questioned them because he knew the killer or killers were close to home. Men he had been raised with, had fished with and socialized with. Not exactly friends or men he would trust in a bind, but people he knew.

Jericho was a small, intimate community. He knew about Miss Eunice, the elderly spinster who ordered her adult toys on a regular basis and her widower neighbor, Charlie Beckett, who watched through the window on scheduled nights of usage. He knew about Tommy Austin and how he whipped his wife on drinking nights, only to sustain a concussion when she got the baseball bat out on him. She had been her softball team's heavy hitter three years in a row.

And there were the parties out by the lake, and the regulars he could count on to keep things calm and safe there. The ones he knew were likely to cause trouble. He knew everyone in the small town, had grown up with them in some form or another, and realizing that several of them were capable of treason, capable of murdering their neighbors in cold blood, had hit him hard. He had always had a decided innocence where his little county was concerned.

Realizing that one of them could commit murder and still function normally had been a bitter pill to swallow. Naïve... He admitted in some ways he had been. His training should have done away with that naiveté long ago. He knew the things men would do for money, for war, just for the hell of it. But seeing it so close to home, so close on the heels of Nine-Eleven, had ripped away any sense of innocence he may have held in the world.

Realizing how corrupt Whittaker was had, perhaps, been the first step. The man was rabid, like a coyote stalking, slinking around in the dark just waiting to rip out the throat of anyone opposing him. And that included Jackson and Becca.

"Whittaker has an old hunting cabin up here somewhere," Jackson said quietly as they pushed farther into the mountain. "I gave Sandor the general location as I remembered it, but from the sound of the helicopter, I could have been a few miles off."

He frowned, trying to place the exact location. It had been years since he had been through this particular area. He had been little more than a teenager, and he and his friends had been more interested in fishing the remote ponds than they were in old man Whittaker's pricey little shack.

"You think he's hiding them there then?" Becca asked as she moved close behind him.

"Seems reasonable," he grunted, angry with himself for his inability to remember the exact location. "The helicopter landed on the other side of this hill, which is about five miles from the location I gave Sandor."

The cell phone he carried with him would be ineffectual where he was now, reception was at zero within these mountains. Which left them on their own. He trusted Becca's abilities as a deputy, but in this situation he knew that the dangers they faced could be more than either of them anticipated. But they had to check this out.

The terrorist threat in America was growing, he knew. His contacts within the Armed Forces and friends who had served in the Middle East since Nine-Eleven reported the growing danger in America, Mexico and Canada. The investigation into the Middle Eastern illegals through Jericho and other states heading into Canada was coming to a head. If they didn't catch them soon, then it would be too late. The information that several highly sought after terrorists were traveling with the families was an added consideration.

"Jackson, you didn't answer me," Becca hissed as they wound their way up the mountain, growing steadily closer to the area he believed the helicopter had landed.

"I know that's where he's hiding them," Jackson sighed, bitterly aware of the fact that he had dropped the ball on this one. He should have checked the cabin months ago.

Whittaker wasn't a nature person, though, so it had never occurred to Jackson to stake out the cabin, or to have Jacob do it. The location of activity so far had been confined away from the cabin, so he hadn't suspected it. Which wasn't a good enough excuse, as far as he was concerned. He was a failure as a sheriff, just as he had been afraid he would be when he was appointed to the post.

"The cabin is a perfect location, Becca," he bit out as they rounded a stand of shoulder-high boulders that looked like sentinels standing watch over the forested valley below. "There's a rough track that leads right into there about a mile from the rest area. It's secluded and not well known. As far as anyone knows, Whittaker sold the damned place years ago. The reason I know different is because I happened on it while doing a search of property taxes on Uncle Tobias' place after his death."

He stopped on the other side of the boulders, leaning against one as he watched Becca plop down on a long, flat boulder nearer the ground. Her breasts were heaving beneath the soft material of her tank top, perspiration glistening on her upper chest and neck.

Tendrils of golden brown had fallen from her ponytail and lay along her graceful neck, tempting him to reach out, to smooth them back. He wasn't about to touch her. The woman was more temptation than was reasonably safe in the best of circumstances.

"So what are we going to do?" She frowned up at him, watching him cautiously.

Jackson sighed. "We're just going to look. If nothing else, we'll have verified proof they are holding them there, which will give our Federal friends a little more leeway in their investigation."

"What about the baby?" she asked him softly.

Worry darkened her eyes and lent a regretful sadness to her expression.

"Becca, the baby is safer than you at the moment." The child of the transported family weighed on her mind, he knew. "And trust me, they paid good money for the transportation, safety and welfare of their people. That child isn't in any danger."

She lowered her head, nodding in acceptance of the answer. That baby had worried her since the day of the accident. Jackson understood why, but he knew in this case, he was most likely right.

"Come on, let's get moving. I want to get off this mountain by nightfall and let Sandor know what the hell is going on."

Chapter Twenty-Five

"We're fucked," Jackson breathed out silently as they watched the cabin from behind a smaller stand of boulders than what he liked.

Laying flat on their stomachs, he and Becca had crawled as close as they dared to watch the activity going on around the large hunting shack. There had to be a dozen Middle Eastern militants running around, unloading the helicopter that had brought in either more inhabitants, or more supplies.

There was Whittaker, in the thick of it shouting out orders. Roby and Martin were there as well, watching the activity going on around them. Jackson narrowed his eyes, watching the foreigners rather than those he already knew. He felt fear strike his heart as he recognized several of them. The terrorists' faces were flashed across every police bulletin going through the nation the year before. Updates were sent through regularly, and he knew priority had been given to capturing several of them.

"What do we do?" Evidently, Becca had realized the danger involved here as well. He could hear the thread of worry in her voice and cursed the moment he had decided to venture up the mountain.

He had left Sandor and Gray a message, so they weren't without recourse. But dammit, the other men wouldn't think to check on them until nightfall. Jackson had assured them that he and Becca could handle this little scouting mission.

"We get the hell out of here," he muttered, motioning her back. "Stay down, Becca, keep behind the boulders until we get back over the edge, then we'll run for it."

They inched back, heading for the small ledge they had worked their way around earlier to get into position to see the cabin. The area they had come through was heavily sheltered, with numerous stands of boulders and large rocks as well as a thick undergrowth. He prayed it would keep them hidden from the men who were no doubt watching for a nosy hunter, or a dumb sheriff. If they were caught, they would die. It was that simple.

Jackson knew Becca was more than aware of this. The merciless intent of the terrorists had been displayed to a nation as it watched in horror. Several of the men now hiding on this mountain had been linked to the planning and details of the terror strike.

"Jackson, this is bad," Becca whispered as they worked their way slowly back along the hard ground. "There's too many there. How the hell do they intend to get them out without being seen?"

"Same way they got them in," he growled. "A few at a time, or in campers or RVs. They're smart and they're dangerous. A deadly combination, baby."

Jackson glanced back, seeing the ledge as it came nearer. They were almost home free. If they could get past that without being sighted, then they had a chance of making it off the small mountain and back to relative safety.

They were inches from just that when the first shot was fired. The bullet just missed Jackson's head, burying in the trunk of the tree beside him instead.

"Fuck! Run!" Jackson screamed out at Becca, terror thudding hard and fast through his bloodstream as a stream of Arabic began to echo through the mountain.

He heard Becca curse, but as he jumped to his feet and cleared the ledge he saw she was already running. But he knew the bastards back at the cabin were running too. Running with semi automatic rifles that could easily take Becca and him out with a properly placed bullet.

179

"Stay close to the trees," he yelled as he came up on her, covering her from behind. "Keep your head low."

Goddamn it, he cursed silently as he spared a quick look back to see several of the terrorists top the ledge and come over it flying.

"Run, Becca!" He pushed her harder, knowing their chances of outrunning the bastards were slim to none, and their weapons hopelessly inferior. It was damned hard to battle automatic rifles with the standard issue police pistol.

Gunfire began to fill the silence of the mountains. Jackson jerked his revolver from its holster, firing back wildly, hoping, if nothing else, to force them to lose any proper aim they had on them. Bullets buried in the trees, ricocheted off boulders and kept them zigzagging, dodging the gunfire as they fought to escape to the relative safety of the vehicle at the bottom of the mountains. God, he had to get Becca out of here.

"Run faster, baby!" he screamed out at her as he glanced back. There had to be half a dozen of those bastards coming down the mountain after them and even more behind them.

The air filled with the sound of gunfire, Arabic curses, and the thunder of his own heart. He pushed Becca harder, screaming at her, urging her to run harder, faster, to get to the safety the caves would afford them. If nothing else, there was communication there, the vehicle. They would have a fighting chance.

He glanced back again, his heart filling his throat as he saw the two men kneeling, raising their rifles. "The trees," he screamed, jerking Becca forward then coming to a halt and slamming her to the ground as a crazed figure rose up in front of them.

He covered Becca's body, staring up at Jacob in amazement as he stood over them, the M16 in his hand spewing out cartridges like a summer storm spills its raindrops.

"Get!" Jacob didn't spare them a glance as he screamed the word.

Jackson jerked Becca to her feet and pushed her back to a dead run. They were nearly there. With Jacob's help and the damned canon-sized weapon he was carrying they at least had a chance now.

"Get to the jeep!" he screamed at Becca. "If we're not in it with you, then get the fuck out of here."

"Like hell," she yelled back, breathless with fear and flight as they tore from the mountain.

"Keep her running, Jack," Jacob yelled out behind them. "We have more coming. Let's get the hell out of here."

"Fuck. Fuck." Jackson pushed harder, hope filling him as they broke the line of trees. "Jeep."

They ran for it as Jackson pushed his hand in his pocket for the keys. It was the last thing he knew. He heard Becca scream, but as he fought the darkness overcoming him, he prayed that if this was his last breath, then Jacob could protect her.

Chapter Twenty-Six

Thank God for Rambo, wherever the hell he came from, Rebecca thought as she ran. Almost there, almost there, she looked back and saw Jackson and Rambo go down. "Jackson!" she screamed. For just a moment she thought her heart stopped. She started toward them when a hand seized her arm and spun her around.

"Not so fast, Rebecca," Todd said with a sneer.

She had no time to think, running on pure emotion and adrenalin. She struck out with her free hand. He caught her and held her against him in an iron grip. Todd had always been strong. She stiffened, twisting against his hold. She distracted him enough to stomp on his instep. He grimaced and cursed but held her firm. His fingers dug into her flesh and he shook her hard, rattling her teeth. "You bastard, you fucking bastard," she snarled and kicked out. Her knee missed his groin by an inch.

"Stop," Todd yelled.

"Like hell." She grunted as he jerked her against him again. She looked up, surprised to find he wasn't talking to her. She turned and saw two Middle Eastern soldiers standing over Jackson and Rambo, guns aimed at their heads.

Panic rose in her and she fought. "No." The word screamed in her brain though it escaped her dry throat as a plea. Todd's grip was unyielding as he squeezed her arms harder; she winced but didn't take her eyes from Jackson.

"I want him alive." He lowered his head and ran his tongue over her ear. "For now."

The caress made her blood boil, and her stomach clench. She wanted to recoil in disgust. Instead she turned her head quick and bit his cheek as hard as she could. She tasted his blood and spat onto the ground. He yelped and pulled away from her. She used the moment to wrench free. She made a mad dash for the gun she knew was in the jeep, only to be caught by Martin and Roby, the two idiots. She twisted futilely against their hold.

Todd stalked toward her. His hand touched his face, and then he looked at the blood on his fingers. She saw the rage in his icy glare. She knew she was outnumbered but she'd be damned if she'd give in or make it easy for them. "Go to hell, you son of a bitch."

Fury flashed in his eyes. He stood over her, fisted his hand in her hair and yanked her head back. "You belong to me. Did you really think I'd stand by and do nothing while you whored yourself out to this dirty country bumpkin?"

Rebecca glared at him, refusing to look away. "I never belonged to you, Todd. Never."

He slapped her hard. Her head snapped back. He waited till she turned back to him. "You did!" he screamed at her. His breath was soughing in and out of his lungs. "You do. And now that hillbilly sheep fucker is going to see. He's going to see that you are mine and then he'll die knowing."

"He knows better," Rebecca said through her teeth.

He kept his gaze locked with hers. Her teeth marks were plain to see in the drying blood on his cheek; a sinister smile slowly curved his lips. She wondered why she hadn't seen this side of him in the beginning. What had ever made her think she could care for this man? Roby and Martin were chuckling, standing too close, their fingers digging into her arms, rubbing against the outside swell of her breasts.

"Those trees over there will be perfect for what I have in mind." Todd gestured with a nod of his head. "Tie them up," he said to the soldiers. "Make sure the sheriff has a good view."

Roby and Martin dragged Rebecca to the place where Todd had directed them. He sauntered up to her with the rope from the jeep, watching the soldiers tie Jackson and Rambo to a tree not far from them. That same smile was still fixed on his face as Todd stepped closer. With a pocketknife he cut the long rope into three shorter pieces. Rebecca struggled, twisting her body, tugging her arms.

"Damn bitch. Be still!" Roby spat.

Todd knelt down and tied a length of rope to each foot. He backed up on his haunches, measuring distances by sight then motioned for them to bring her forward. He stood, pulling the ropes, and her feet came out from under her. Roby and Martin dropped her. The breath whooshed from her lugs as her back hit the hard packed dirt. Martin planted his booted foot on her chest. She fought for breath as Roby knelt quickly and grabbed her arms, jerking them over her head. He tied them together while Todd and one of the soldiers each took a leg. Rebecca kicked and bucked. Todd just laughed as he spread her open, tying them wide apart.

"What the hell?" Whittaker was out of breath and sweating like the pig he was. "Have you lost your fuckin' mind, Lawrence? Just kill 'em and be done with it."

Todd scowled at the man. "I'll handle this the way I see fit. If you can't stomach it then take the men and go back to the cabin."

They glared at each other for a tense moment, until finally Whittaker waved a hand. "Fuck it. Do what ya want. The nosy little bitch and her fuck buddy had it comin'." Whittaker turned and motioned to the soldiers to leave.

Todd knelt between her legs and began cutting her clothes from her body. She grit her teeth, pulling against the ropes that dug into her wrists and ankles. Her stressed joints burned as she bucked and jerked. Rebecca knew what was going to happen. She refused to think about the fact that Whittaker, Roby and Martin stood to the side, their arms crossed, their eyes glassy waiting for the show.

She shuddered with revulsion as she watched Todd. His hands roamed over her, cutting away her shirt, her bra. She held her breath as the knife lightly circled her nipple. Hating that they involuntarily tightened from the feel of the cold metal, she swallowed the knot of fear and anger that rose inside her, threatening to choke her. He sat back and let his gaze travel over her naked body hungrily, predatorily. "Wake him up," he said with a grin.

She wanted to cringe but she didn't. She faced him, hated him with everything in her for what he was about to do to her, to Jackson, to their relationship. She'd feed on that hate. Todd's hand replaced the knife, trailing over her breast. He squeezed. Her stomach lurched and she swallowed. "You disgust me," she snarled.

His gaze locked with hers, his features contorting as his fist plowed into her jaw. Pain flashed through her skull as her head bounced off the ground. Breathing deeply through her nose she tried to resist the need to puke. Glaring at him she worked her jaw to assure herself that it was still intact. An ominous growl reached her ears and she knew it came from Jackson.

"You stupid whore," Todd grunted. He turned, facing Jackson. Rebecca clenched her teeth as Todd shoved his fingers inside her, sending sharp pain radiating through her. "This is my cunt. I'm taking it back. You're going to watch," he snarled and began unbuckling his pants.

She turned her head then. Jackson was watching her, his gaze locking with hers. Fury reflected in his hard, cold eyes. He strained against the ropes binding him, his expression murderous. The muscle in his jaw jumped, the muscles and veins in his neck bulged.

If they did somehow live through this it would never be the same. Once Todd raped her, Jackson would never look at her the way he once had. She would be lost to him. The only man she ever loved. No matter what Todd did to her, her heart, her mind, her soul would belong to Jackson. Only him. She couldn't help the tears that fell across the bridge of her nose. So many things she never said. "Jackson." She mouthed his name.

Chapter Twenty-Seven

"No! Goddamn you, Lawrence!" Jackson screamed, every bone and muscle in his body rioting as agony flashed through his soul. Lawrence was daring to touch her. He would kill the son of the bitch; if he had to do it from the grave, he would kill him.

Becca. His Becca. God, why hadn't he told her he loved her, told her what she meant to him. He saw the bastard touching her, as he felt the tears that radiated from his soul, searing his eyes as hers fell along her bruised face. Fucking bastard, he was going to kill him. He would kill him with his bare hands. He fought the ropes at his wrists, refusing to watch what Todd was doing to her. He kept his eyes locked with Becca's trying to show her, to love her, to give her the strength he knew she would need to get through this.

God help him, he prayed. Please God, don't let that bastard rape her. He felt his skin breaking beneath the ropes, felt the moisture of his own blood and couldn't stop. He had to get free. He had to help her. Becca would never survive such brutality.

Jacob had called in the State boys. Jackson knew that. How Jacob knew what the hell was going on Jackson didn't know, but he knew help was coming. He just had to distract him, had to delay him.

"Lawrence, you don't want to do this," he screamed out again as Becca flinched, her eyes dazed as Todd's mouth moved between her naked, helpless thighs.

Lawrence stopped, turned his head back to sneer at Jackson.

"She tastes good, doesn't she, Jackson?" he called out. "Our little Rebecca gets so hot and wet when you're eating her tight pussy. Does she beg you like she used to beg me?"

A red haze of rage went over Jackson at those words.

Becca mouthed the word "no," repeated it over and over, as though she needed to deny his claim.

"Only a fool takes an unwilling woman, Todd." He fought to hold the other man's attention. "You know Becca, man. She'll kill you when she gets free. And if she doesn't, then by God I will."

"Rebecca!" Lawrence screamed as he came to his feet. "Her name is Rebecca, you stupid sheep fucker. She's not a pokey hick Becca."

"Then Rebecca will kill you," he snarled bitterly. "Your ego is making an ass of you, Lawrence. She doesn't want you."

Lawrence glanced down at Becca's bound body, watching her struggle as Jackson fought to get free.

"Doesn't matter," he sneered. "I'll take her anyway and you'll watch. Watch as I fuck her and as I kill her. And you'll die knowing I was the last man to have her. That I took back what belonged to me."

"No. Stop." Jackson's lips curled back from his teeth as Lawrence went to his knees again, his mouth latching onto the flesh between Becca's thighs as she screamed out in pain.

The sound tore through him like a thousand blades. Her eyes closed as she strained against the ropes, fighting like a demon, demented, unable to accept what was happening to her.

"I love you, Becca!" He screamed out the vow as he fought his own ropes. "I love you, baby."

He screamed out her name again, struggling, fighting the ropes as terror lit a fury inside his soul that threatened to drive him insane. He screamed out Lawrence's name again, heaving against the ropes that restrained him like an enraged bull.

Then he heard the disgusted hiss behind him. "Shut the fuck up before they see me, you moron."

The female voice was filled with anger, as she tucked a gun into his hand. "Hang on, I'll cut you loose."

Jackson started praying. He watched in horror as Lawrence's mouth came away from Becca's thighs, a sneer on his lips as he rose to his feet, his hands going to the crotch of his pants to pull his penis free. Then he glanced at Jackson. The knife sliced through the rope as Lawrence's eyes widened.

Jackson wasted no time. With Becca's screams still echoing in his ears, he brought the gun around as he went to his knee and fired. He took out Lawrence and Martin, each with a shot to the forehead, as four State Trooper vehicles screamed into the clearing. Then Roby and Whittaker fell as Jacob came out firing as well. Jackson swung around then for the three terrorists.

He shot low, taking out a knee, an ankle, but Jacob went for the heart. The third was dead before he hit the ground. Before he could think Jackson was on his feet and running for Becca.

The woman who had cut him loose, obviously the one Jacob had at his cabin weeks before, was already cutting her loose and kicking Lawrence's lifeless body to the side.

"Becca." He caught her as she began scrambling hysterically away from Lawrence's body, her desperate sobs cutting into his heart as he jerked his T-shirt off and forced it over her head.

She fought him as he dressed her, strangled cries pouring from her throat as she begged him to let her wash. To let her clean Lawrence's touch from her body.

"It's okay, baby." He pulled her into his arms as the hysteria began to slowly ease. His arms tightened around her, rocking her as State Troopers poured into the area and an official helicopter flew low overhead.

"Oh God. Jackson." She clutched at him then, burying her face against his chest as she shuddered in reaction. "I was so scared. I was so scared."

Her voice was hoarse, dazed and shocky as her nails bit into the skin of his shoulders. She fought to get closer to him as his arms tightened around her, his body bending over her, sheltering her, holding her as close as possible.

"It's over, baby." He felt tears on his own cheeks, his muscles still taut, tight as he fought his own reaction. He held her tighter, rocking her, holding her close, his eyes closing as emotion washed over him. "I love you, Becca," he whispered as she finally stilled against him. "Do you understand me, baby? I knew it a week ago and didn't tell you. I knew it when you were sixteen and was too terrified to accept it. I love you." He rocked her, whispered the strangled words in her ear as he felt his own tears dampen his cheeks.

So close, he had come so close to losing her, and she hadn't even known that she held his heart and soul. He swore that not a day would go by now that she didn't know, that she didn't hear the words from his lips, the feeling in his touch.

Hell had erupted around them. Troopers were yelling orders back and forth, and Arabic curses filled the air as more sirens joined the melee going on around them. Jackson lifted Becca in his arms and carried her to the stream. There he held her as she washed, as she cried and fought to get past the horror of what Lawrence had done to her.

She had known him, and though she hadn't loved him, hadn't really liked him, she had never believed that such evil existed in him. That innocence had been stripped from her, and though Jackson knew she would survive it intact, she would never forget it.

He helped her dress after drying her carefully, thankful that she was slowly calming down, the color coming back into her face. He had hidden her in the cave, carrying her to the farthest corner of it, allowing her the privacy she needed to come to grips with it. Outside, Sandor was calling his name, his voice fierce, imperative. There were reports to make and a briefing to get through, but Jackson hadn't observed the rules since taking office, he figured now wasn't a hell of a good time to start. They would get what they needed when he got around to giving it to them.

"Jackson." Her voice, soft, husky from the tears she had shed earlier drew his attention to her.

He turned around on the crate he had been sitting on, watching as she came from the shadows of the back of the cave. She was dressed in jeans and his shirt. Her wet hair brushed back, her face no longer so pale. She walked into his arms.

Without hesitation, without the fear he had worried would be there, she came to him.

"I want to go home, Jackson," she whispered. "Take me home and love me. I want this memory wiped away, Jackson."

She sounded fierce, angry, his Becca. He listened to the commotion outside, thought again of all that needed to be done.

"We'll have to sneak away," he whispered with a smile of anticipation. "They're looking for us."

"Let 'em look." Her lips caressed his neck as her arms tightened around him. "Let's go home, Jackson. You promised me the nightstick. I think I'm ready now."

Epilogue

Rebecca whimpered as she watched Jackson watch her from lowered lids while he licked and sucked her toes. She never knew the nerves in her toes were directly connected to the nerves in her cunt. She sighed as his tongue moved to her ankle, her calf, the back of her knee. He paused there nibbling, sucking, driving her crazy.

His silver eyes glittered with naughtiness as his hands caressed her. He looked up at her through dark lashes. "Feel good?"

"Mm hmm." She closed her eyes and submerged herself in Jackson, his scent, his touch.

He sucked at her inner thigh and she gasped, liquid arousal spreading through the sensitive folds of her pussy. She parted her legs for him, the short stubble on his cheeks rubbing against her swollen lips. Her blood heated as he kissed her there, his tongue delving inside, drawing her juices through the narrow slit.

She felt him move away and lean over the side of the bed. Her eyes sprung open to see him holding a long black nightstick. A slow smile spread across her face to match his. "I was joking," she said.

He lifted a brow. "I wasn't."

She gave him a dubious look. "Jackson…"

"Trust me, baby. I will never, ever hurt you." He nestled himself between her thighs again and plunged his tongue inside her, drawing it up and over her clit. He lapped at her, making her moan and writhe. He spread her apart, his thumbs rubbing over the sensitive folds as he pressed the nightstick against her entrance. She felt her muscled walls clench, sucking it inside as his tongue circled and rasped over her swelling clit.

"Rub your breasts, baby, rub those gorgeous berries for me," Jackson mumbled, his voice vibrating against her cunt. "Damn, I wish I had more hands."

"Me too," she panted as she cupped her own breasts, rolling her nipples between her fingers.

He chuckled against her and the nightstick sunk a little deeper. She groaned and arched up, taking as much of it as she could.

Rebecca cried out at the sharp pleasure that fired through her. He gave her as much of the nightstick as she could take, then drew it out slowly as he took her clit between his lips, sucked gently, giving it little flicks of his tongue.

"Oh God, Jackson," she screamed as he sucked harder, thrusting the nightstick in and out. She bucked up as the climax slammed through her.

He kissed his way up her body, pausing at her navel and her breasts. His mouth closed over one pert nipple. His hand molded the other breast, she cried out as his thumb rasped over it. The ripples cascading over her didn't have a chance to subside before they grew again. Jackson slid up her body, his mouth possessing her, muffling her moans as he entered her in one smooth stroke.

The weight of Jackson covering her body, pressing her into the soft mattress, felt more than wonderful. He kissed her bruised cheek, whispering sweet things in her ear. His hand supported her head as his hard body, slick with sweat, slid over hers, the length of his cock moving inside her with long, slow thrusts. With every stroke, waves of pleasure flowed over her, each one deeper, more powerful, pushing her toward her climax.

Rebecca wrapped her legs around his and tilted her hips, taking him deeper, reveling in the power of his desire for her. Feeling his body tremble, the muscles in his back ripple as he struggled to take it slow, intensified her own passion. Her hands traveled downward to grip his tight ass, pulling him in deeper, arching her back. She whimpered, not sure if she could take this pace much longer. The sensual ache emanating through her body made her yearn for release but at the same time the friction of Jackson's substantial cock slowly pumping felt so good, she wanted it to last forever.

He withdrew slowly then plunged into her. She arched up her head, fell back on a cry. "Becca. God, Becca I need..." He moaned against her neck, sucking and licking as he picked up the pace.

"Yes," she cried as he grasped her hips and rose to his knees. She gasped and bucked up, her hips pistoning up to meet his driving thrusts. "Jack...Jackson," she cried breathlessly. His ravenous mouth moved over her jaw, her neck, her mouth, their tongues tangling, lips nibbling. "I love you, Jackson. Oh God, I love you so much."

"Becca. I love you, baby," he croaked.

She wrapped her legs around his hips and her arms around his neck and hung on as sensations burst along every nerve cell. Jackson stiffened and plunged deep inside her, calling her name, his body trembling. She moaned and cried though her orgasm as it swept over her in long undulating waves. Jackson groaned, filling her with hot jets of his cream.

He rolled over taking her with him. She lay on his chest listening to his heart pound.

* * * * *

"Time to get up." Jackson nosed aside Becca's hair from her nape and kissed the sensitive skin gently.

Sleeping on her stomach, her body relaxed and flushed, she was a temptation he was hard pressed to ignore. Getting her back to the house after the arrest and general cleanup of the traffickers and terrorist families had been hell. Unfortunately, Sandor had caught them trying to sneak away, and had delayed them by several hours. But the cleanup and reports had been made and they were finally allowed to head home.

Home. It had been a long time since any place had been home.

"Becca," he whispered against her neck again, his hand moving slowly over the curves of her rear as he pressed her to wake up. He had plans, and they had an appointment, one he wasn't about to cancel. He had spent the last hour setting it up, and getting everything ready. There was no room for excuses, no way for her to wiggle out of it.

"Wha..." she mumbled into the pillows, trying to burrow deeper in the mattress to escape.

"Wake up, baby," he chuckled as she scooted away from him.

"Go 'way," she growled, pulling the pillow over her head.

Jackson pulled the pillow away, amazed as he always was, how his heart could just soften, melt with the smallest things she did. She amazed him, captivated him, made him so damned horny that half the time he was in a haze of lust. And he loved her. Loved her in ways he didn't think was possible.

"Becca, this is important. Wake up." He pulled the blankets from her as she tried to burrow under them once again.

She flopped over on her back. Her firm breasts peaked with those pretty little berry nipples, making his mouth water. Her eyes were narrowed in warning.

"The house on fire?" she asked huskily.

"No." He shook his head, his gaze going to those perfect breasts once again.

She cleared her throat. "You got produce or strange articles you're wanting to try out?" Her eyes gleamed in interest.

"Nope." He stilled the grin wanting to form at his mouth.

She frowned in disappointment. "Oh. Well, I'm going back to sleep." She went to flip back over.

"Oh no, you don't." He laughed, gripping her arms and pulling her up in the bed. "Get showered and dressed. I laid out that pretty cream-colored dress that was hanging in your closet, and everything else you need. We're in a hurry."

She grumbled under her breath, pushing her hair out of her eyes as she stared up at him. "What's the hurry? A dress? Where the hell are we going that I need a dress?"

"Church." The word hung in the air around them as she shook her head in confusion.

"Today's Sunday? Are you sure?"

"Today's Friday."

"Are you trying to deliberately confuse me?" She frowned then, the sleep slowly clearing from her eyes. "Why are we going to church, Jackson?"

"To get married."

"Oh, that's okay th−" Her eyes widened, blinked, as she swallowed tightly. "Married?"

"I won't let you back out of it either, Becca," he warned her fiercely. "We're getting married."

"Married?" she whispered, shaking her head. "When did you propose?"

"Propose? No way." He shook his head, fighting his irrational fear that if he didn't marry her now, then something would happen, some way, somehow, someone would destroy the chance.

Jackson wasn't a fool. Had Lawrence managed to actually rape her, then Becca would have healed from it. She would have left him, would have fought any chance they had of surviving it together. If he tied her to him, and did it now, then no matter what happened, she was committed. She was his.

"Jackson." She shook her head. "You're supposed to propose." She protested as he pulled her from the bed. "You know? Wine, a ring, all that good stuff?"

"Rings are at the church, we'll celebrate with wine afterward. Now shower." He pulled back the door and began adjusting the water.

"Jackson, I want to marry you." He stilled, his heart lodging in his throat as he sat down slowly on the edge of the tub.

He stared up at her, his heart breaking as he remembered her screams. She had screamed out his name, begging him to help her. If Angie hadn't been there, there had been no way he could have gotten to her in time.

"I can't lose you, Becca," he whispered then, jerking her to him, his face buried at her stomach as he fought the emotion surging inside him. "Do you understand me? No matter what happens, no matter what anyone else does, you're my heart. You're my world."

"What time is the ceremony?" she asked softly, sliding down until she rested on her knees, staring up at him with a wicked glint in her eye.

"Two hours." He touched her face, marveling at how deeply he loved her.

"So when did you intend to do the actual proposal?" She arched a brow curiously.

Jackson grinned. "During the honeymoon."

She shook her head, laughing up at him then. The sheer pleasure and love he saw in her filled his world.

"Marry me, Becca," he whispered then, needing to know it was what she needed as well.

"Yes, Jackson. I'll marry you."

He would have spoken. Hell, he had every intention of whooping in joy. But a second later her mouth closed over the head of his erection, sucking the breath from him as she began to suck his flesh deep into her mouth.

Damn, his Pixie Pest was a daily surprise. A treasure. His heart.

About the author:

Lora Leigh is a 36-year-old wife and mother living in Kentucky. She dreams in bright, vivid images of the characters intent on taking over her writing life, and fights a constant battle to put them on the hard drive of her computer before they can disappear as fast as they appeared. Lora's family, and her writing life co-exist, if not in harmony, in relative peace with each other. An understanding husband is the key to late nights with difficult scenes, and stubborn characters. His insights into human nature, and the workings of the male psyche provide her hours of laughter, and innumerable romantic ideas that she works tirelessly to put into effect.

Lora welcomes mail from readers. You can write to her c/o Ellora's Cave Publishing at 1337 Commerce Drive, Suite 13, Stow OH 44224.

Also by Lora Leigh:

TEMPTING THE BEAST

Book 1 in the Feline Breeds series

By Lora Leigh

Preview

CHAPTER ONE

Washington D.C.

"This story is mine." Merinus stared down her family of seven brothers and one father, her voice firm, her determination unwavering.

She knew she didn't present an imposing figure. At five feet five inches, it was damned hard to convince the males of her family, all over six feet, that she was serious about anything. But in this one instance, she knew she had no other choice.

"Don't you think this is a little bit much for you to take on, Squirt?" Caleb, editor-in-chief of the National Forum and her second oldest brother, smirked with an edge of superiority.

Merinus refused to give into his baiting. She looked down the long table, directly into her father's thoughtful expression. John Tyler was the one to convince, not his moron upstarts.

"I've worked hard, Dad, I can do this." She fought to put the steely determination in her voice that she often heard her oldest brother use. "I deserve this chance."

She was twenty-four years old, the youngest child in a family of eight and the only daughter. She hated makeup, despised dresses and social functions and she heard often how she was a disappointment to the female race, according to her brothers. She wanted to be a journalist; she wanted to make a difference. She wanted to stand before the man whose picture lay on the table before her and see if his eyes were really that brilliant amber. Perhaps she was more woman than they knew.

She was obsessed. Merinus silently admitted to it, and knew she would play hell trying to hide it. From the moment she had seen the picture of the man in question, she had been nervous, panicky, terrified that his enemies would get to him before she could present her father's offer.

"What makes you think you're the best person for this job, Merinus?" Her father leaned forward, clasping his hands on the table before him, his blue eyes serious, thoughtful as he watched her.

"Because I'm a woman." She allowed herself a small smile. "You put that much testosterone in the same room with just one of the behemoth seven here, and you'll have an automatic refusal. But he would listen to a woman."

"Listen to her, or try to seduce her?" one of her other brothers questioned harshly. "This idea is unacceptable."

Merinus kept her eyes on her father and prayed Kane, the oldest brother would keep his mouth shut. Their father listened to him where she was concerned and if he decided it was too dangerous, then there was no way John Tyler would allow her to go.

"I know how to be careful," she told him softly. "You and Kane trained me well. I want this chance. I deserve it."

And if she didn't get it, then she would take it on her own. She knew her brothers couldn't make contact, but she could. She suppressed a shiver at the thought. Some would say the man wasn't even human. A genetic experiment conceived in a test tube, carried to term by a surrogate and inheriting the genes of the animal his DNA had been altered with. A man with all the instincts and hunting abilities of a lion. A perfectly human looking male. A man bred to be a savage killer.

Merinus had read the notes, experiments and the thirty-year journal of the scientist who carried him within her body. Dr. Maria Morales had been a friend of her father's in college. It was she who had the box ready to be delivered to John in the event of her death. It was his decision who would carry out the woman's last request.

He was to find her surrogate son at the location she had given. Help him defeat the secret Genetics Council by convincing him to come forward, making a way for him to find safety. She had enough proof to get them digging. Kane had done the rest. They had names of the Council, proof of their involvement, everything but the man they created.

"This is too dangerous to trust to her," Caleb argued again. The others were silent, but Merinus knew they would voice their opinions soon enough.

Merinus took a deep breath.

"I get the story, or I follow whichever moron in this room gets it. You won't have a chance."

"This coming from the woman who refuses to wear makeup or a dress?" another brother piped in with a snicker. "Honey, you don't have what it takes."

"It doesn't take being a whore," she bit out furiously, turning on the youngest brother. "It's simple logic, dunce. A woman, whether in pants or a dress will draw more attention from a man than any other man will. He's careful, he doesn't trust easily. Maria's notes state that plainly. He won't trust another man. The basic male threat."

"And he could very well be just as dangerous as he was created to be," Caleb argued for Gray as he swiped his fingers through his short brown hair. "Dammit, Merinus, you have no business even wanting to be anywhere near this bastard."

Merinus took a deep breath. She lowered her eyes, staring down at the bleak loneliness reflected through glossy paper. His eyes mesmerized her, even in the picture. There were decades of sadness reflected there. He was thirty years old now, single, alone. A man without a family or even a race to call his own. How terrible it must be, and to be hunted as well was a tragedy.

"I won't stay here," she said loud enough for them all to hear. "I'll follow whoever goes out there and I won't let you hound him."

The silence was heavy now. Merinus could feel eight sets of eyes on her, varying degrees of disapproval reflected in their expressions.

"I'll go with her. I can handle the research part, Merinus can make contact." Kane's voice had Merinus jerking her head up in surprise.

Shock echoed along her body as she realized that the brother who suffocated her the most was actually willing to help her in this. It was hard to believe. Kane was arrogant and ninety percent of the time, the world's worst jerk. He was an ex-Special Forces commander as bossy as any man ever born.

For the first time she looked directly at him. His expression was cool, but his eyes were angry. Deep and hot with fury, the dark blue orbs met hers without their usual light of teasing mockery. The intensity in his look almost frightened her. He wasn't angry with her, she could tell, but Kane was pissed. And a pissed Kane was not a good thing.

Merinus was aware of her father sitting back in his seat, watching the eldest son now with surprise.

"You've put a lot of time in this already, Kane," John remarked. "Six months at least. I thought you would be ready for a rest?"

Kane glanced at his father, shrugging his shoulders with a tight movement.

"I want to see it through. I'll be close enough to help her out if she needs me, but also able to do the research that could be too damned dangerous for her. If she can be ready to leave tonight, then we can do this her way."

"I'll be ready." Her response was instantaneous. "Just tell me what time."

"Be ready at four. We have an eight-hour drive ahead of us and I want to do some recon before morning. Damn good thing you don't care if you chip a few nails, brat, because you'll be doing just that."

He came to his feet abruptly as the men around him erupted into a furious argument. Merinus could only watch him silently, amazed at his decision. What the hell was up with this?

He ignored the heated protests of his other brothers. The arguments of Merinus' safety, the lack of assurance that 'some damned hybrid animal' wouldn't infect her. Merinus rolled her eyes, then bit her lip nervously as Kane's face tightened into a mask of dangerous fury. His eyes went dead. She couldn't describe it any other way. As though no life or light resided inside him. It was a scary look.

The room silenced. No one but no one messed with Kane when he looked like that.

"Be ready, baby sister," he said evenly as he passed by her. "And if you pack one damned dress or a single tube of lipstick, then I'll lock your ass up in your bedroom."

"Ahh, Kane," she whined sarcastically. "There goes my luggage quota. Asshole." He knew better than to think she would pack either one.

"Keep your nose clean, brat." He flicked the ends of her long brown hair as he walked by her. "I'll pick you up this evening."

CHAPTER TWO

Sandy Hook, KY

That was not a sight for virgin eyes. Merinus trained her binoculars on the vision below her, stretched out in the warming rays of the sun, as naked as a man could be and more than a little aroused. That gorgeous, heavily veined shaft of male flesh rose a good eight inches—no less, could be more—from the base below his flat abdomen. It was thick and long and mouth-wateringly tempting. She blew out a hard breath, lying flat on the rock she had found, the only viewpoint into the small sheltered back yard. She couldn't take her eyes off him.

Callan Lyons was tall. At least six feet, four inches, muscular, broad chested and narrow hipped, with powerful thighs and the most gorgeous damned legs she had ever seen. This just wasn't a sight that a nice, prudish little journalist like herself should be seeing. It could give a girl ideas. Ideas like how it would feel to lie next to him, rub over him, kiss that smooth, golden skin. She shivered at the thought.

She and Mr. Lyons had been playing an amusing little game for over a week now. She pretended not to know him, who he was, where he could be found, and he pretended she wasn't snooping around town asking questions about him and his deceased mother and where he lived. It had gone so far as direct conversation several times. Like she hadn't come prepared, she thought mockingly. Papers, notes, memos, pictures, the whole nine yards. She had studied the man for weeks before demanding this story.

She still couldn't believe Kane had stood by her and brought her with him to contact Callan. Not that he wasn't breathing down her neck half the time. He would be now if he hadn't had to run back to D.C. to talk to a scientist they thought might have been involved with the original experiments. And Merinus was supposed to be finding out about Callan's mother and making contact with the elusive object of her fascination.

So here she was, the story of her life, and instead of the investigative reporting she should be doing on the man below, she was watching him sun himself. But what a sight. Tanned, muscular skin. Long, golden brown hair, the color of the lion that was supposedly infused into his DNA structure. A strong, bold face, gorgeous, almost savage in its planes and angles. And lips, full male lips with just a hint of a merciless curve. She wanted to kiss those lips. She wanted to start with his lips and kiss and lick her way down. Across that broad chest, the hard, flat stomach to the erection rising from between his tanned thighs. She licked her lips at the thought.

She jerked as she felt her cell phone vibrating at her hips. She grimaced impatiently. She knew who it was. It had to be her oldest, most aggravating brother.

"What, Kane?" she hissed as she flipped the phone open and settled it against her ear. She was rather proud that her eyes never once strayed from all that male glory below.

"It could have been Dad," Kane reminded her, his voice flat and hard.

"It could have been the Pope too, but we know the averages on that one," she muttered.

"Bitch," he growled almost affectionately.

"Why Kane, how sweet," she simpered. "I love you too, asshole."

There was a brief chuckle over the line, making her smile in response.

"How's the story going?" His voice turned serious, too serious.

"It's getting there. I have an appointment later today with a woman willing to talk about the mother. She was murdered in her own home. Dad doesn't know that."

Maria Morales, known as Jennifer Lyons in the small Southern California town had died at the hands of an attacker, not a thief or a random victim, but someone who wanted only blood.

"What do you think you're going to learn researching the mother?" Kane asked her. "You need proof on the son, Merrie, don't forget that."

"I know what I'm after, big shot," she bit out. "But to get to the son, I need information. Besides, someone's trying to give me the runaround on Morales. You know how I hate that."

There was a puzzle there, just as big a puzzle as the one stretched out on the deck below her. Sweet Heaven. She watched as his hand moved to his scrotum, not to scratch as she assumed, but to caress, stroke. There went her damned blood pressure.

"I'm research, remember?" he bit out. "You are just contact."

"Well, I can do some of both," she hissed.

There was a weary sigh across the line.

"Have you made contact with Lyons yet? Offered him the deal Dad has set up?" Yeah, the deal of a lifetime, show yourself, tell your story for us, and we'll make you famous. Fuck your life. She hadn't liked that deal to begin with but she knew it was the only one Callan was ever likely to receive that would provide any measure of security.

"Not yet. Getting there." She fought to breathe evenly as his hand clasped the base of that thick cock and he began stroking all that firm, wonderful flesh.

He was going to masturbate. Incredulity flared through her system, especially her vagina, at the realization. Right here before her eyes the man was going to masturbate. She couldn't believe it. His hand barely circled the broad shaft, moving slow and easy, almost lazily from tip to base.

She felt the flesh between her thighs heat. The muscles of her vagina clenched, moistened, her womb contracted as sensual heat speared her body like a bolt of lightning. Her nipples hardened, ached. Her body became so sensitive she could feel the breeze caressing her bare arms now, like the stroke of a ghostly lover.

Gracious, was this how men felt when they watched women masturbate? No wonder they liked it so well. Long, broad fingers stroked over his cock from tip to base, the fingers of his other hand gripped the sac beneath, massaging it in time to the stimulation of the other hand. Where was a damned breeze when she needed it? She was due to overheat any minute.

"Hurry, Merinus, you don't have the rest of your life," Kane grunted. "The bastard has mercenaries stalking him. I can't keep your ass covered forever, you know. I have three more days here, and Dad's pitching fits over you being there by yourself."

Yeah, mercenaries. She blinked as she watched those hands cover the thick head of his own erection, the tips of his fingers caressing the area just underneath. She licked her lips, wishing she was there helping him. She was a doomed virgin.

"I'll hurry, I promise," she muttered. "Now let me get off here so I can get some damned work done. I don't have time to bullshit with you all day."

She heard him sigh roughly.

"Check in soon. You wait too long to call," he accused her.

"Why should I? You call everyday instead," she told him absently. "I have to go, Kane. Got work to do. Chat with ya later, hon."

She heard him curse as she disconnected and tucked the little phone back into its handy case at her hip. Good Lord, she was going to have a stroke. Cat boy was playing his cock like a finely tuned instrument now. She could have sworn she saw the head pulse, throb. His hips arched, then a thick stream of creamy semen erupted from the tip, splattering on that hard abdomen and coating the rough hand.

"Oh man, let me taste," she whispered, unable to take her eyes from the sight.

Then he stretched, his eyes opening. She breathed in sharply as their gazes connected, a self-satisfied smile stretching across those wonderful lips. Of course, he couldn't know she was there, she assured herself. It just wasn't possible. Was it?

About the author:

As a young impassioned girl with a vivid imagination, Veronica Chadwick learned to express her thoughts, ideas and emotions through writing. As an adult she dabbled restlessly here and there with both poetry and prose. Finally, Veronica was introduced to Ellora's Cave and Erotica/Romantica. Her hot, rugged heroes and headstrong, vibrant heroines took control, helping her focus her energies and she knew without a doubt she had found her perfect niche.

In addition to writing, Veronica divides her time between home schooling her two gorgeous children, spending time with her wonderful husband who thankfully loves to cook and caring for their three cats and one very sweet beagle. Veronica has very eclectic tastes in just about every aspect of her life. Though she needs and cherishes all the quiet alone time she can manage to steal, she loves spending time with friends and chatting over a great cup of coffee.

Veronica welcomes mail from readers. You can write to her c/o Ellora's Cave Publishing at 1337 Commerce Drive, Suite 13, Stow OH 44224.

Also by Veronica Chadwick

The Warlord's Gift
Educating Mr. Winters

THE WARLORD'S GIFT

By Veronica Chadwick

Preview

Draven moved effortlessly, pushing though the dark branches and clinging vines in his path. Weary, hungry and annoyed he paid no heed to the two men who fought to keep up with his long strides. After tracking the thieving Gavril half the night, Draven and his men had lost him. The wicked elf had all but vaporized into the fog, cackling like an old woman gone mad. Damn this oppressive fog and damn that little imp, Draven thought. The elf's clever escape was only a temporary reprieve. When he caught the greedy toad he'd make him plead for mercy.

"Mason and I will gather some men when we arrive home." Armond spoke, breaking the tense silence. "We can have this issue dealt with before dawn. You have matters of more pressing need to attend to without having to hunt down these blasted elves."

"No." Draven's tone matched his dangerous mood.

"Use some common sense, Draven. You know Armond is right." Any other man would be a fool to argue; nevertheless, Mason knew his cousin better than anyone. Although he was neither as tall nor as big as Draven, he wasn't short. He was solidly built, heavily ·muscled and had been a challenging competitor.

"There's the meeting with the Endarian Overseer," Mason continued. "And you must prepare for your wedding at the end of the moon phase..." Draven cut him a sharp look. Mason smiled at Draven's grunt of disgust. "...or devise a way to avoid it."

Draven didn't break his stride. "All right, but not this night. The fog is growing too thick. Go at sunrise; the elf situation will hold till then. We all know where Gavril will hole up. Once you've found the elves and dealt with them, bring Gavril to me. The little demon will be sorry his mother and father ever met."

Draven stopped abruptly, sensing the presence before he heard it. Waves of fear, oily and acrid, came from beyond the darkness and assaulted his senses. Lifting a hand to stop the men and warn them to silence, he pivoted to his left and stood motionless. They heard the crackling underbrush, a thud and a muffled cry. Draven moved toward the sound and then stopped.

Through the cold gray mist that clung like damp gauze and the musty scent of moss and earth, he sensed a white-hot pain and panic. Knowing an injured beast could be more dangerous than a fit one, his muscles tensed, his hand gripping the hilt of his sword. Cautiously he moved through the dense vegetation that opened into a clearing. There, in a heap, lay a dark form crumpled across a fallen dead oak. A pale feminine hand reached out.

Perplexed at the unusual intensity of the emotions he received from her, his brows furrowed. Draven felt her nausea, the swelling pain in her leg and the tremendous ache that spread throughout her body. She lifted her head and looked up at him. Her face was shrouded in shadows but he couldn't look away. He felt her fear growing and knew the three of them were frightening her further.

He'd never sensed anyone or anything so sharply. The force of what was inside her threatened to overwhelm him. Great Creator, he thought in frustration, why was he cursed with this affliction? He had not the time to help every injured stray and weak little broken bird that fell across his path. He'd be better off to leave the girl here and let fate have her.

Even as the thought occurred to him he moved to her, knelt, and picked her up. She bit her lip; he'd felt the little twinge of pain. It amazed him that her senses were so overloaded she hadn't even noticed. In his arms, her body trembled with pain, panic, cold and a fear so dark Draven held his breath and bit back an oath.

He shared his warmth with her and she looked up at him, breathing heavily. Mesmerized by what he saw in her cobalt eyes, he held her gaze until her eyelids fluttered closed and her head rested limply against his shoulder. Pain enveloped him in hard unyielding pulses then faded away. It was good that she had passed out, Draven thought, his eyes narrowing as he absorbed her suffering.

Draven turned and started for home. Mason and Armond glanced at each other then reluctantly started after him.

Armond spoke first. "Let me take her to the temple, Draven. They will help her there. More than likely she lost her way in the fog."

"Yes," Mason agreed. "We can send someone to see that she is well cared for."

Draven pushed forward, ignoring them. Anger and an odd possessiveness rose in him.

Mason put his hand on Draven's shoulder. "Stop. Please, cousin, listen to us."

Draven stopped and glared at Mason.

"This is foolish," Mason continued, defying the unmistakable warning in Draven's eyes. "You can't attend to this woman now. You are king; you have too many demands on your time and attention at present." His voice softened. "Leave her to the wise men. They will treat her spirit as well as her body."

"Someone may be looking for her." Armond stepped forward. His green eyes full of concern, he held out his arms. "Delegate this problem, Draven. Give her to me. I will see that she gets the best care."

Draven's voice sounded more like a growl. "She is badly hurt, on my land, my subject. She is my problem. I will see to her care. Personally. You will stand down, Armond."

Armond held up his hands in a defensive gesture and backed away.

"For the love of Iybae, we only mean to help you see reason." Mason stepped closer and lowered his voice. "Block her, Draven. Shut it down."

Draven glanced sharply at Mason and moved on, doing his best to ignore him. He didn't think he could block her if he wanted to. Knowing that only added to his frustration and concern. No, he wouldn't let the girl out of his sight. She was decidedly more than she appeared. Where she had come from was unknown and he sensed a power within her he couldn't quite discern yet. He frowned at the thought. She was a threat to him and his people…a potentially fatal one.

Mason sighed and waved his arm, following behind. "You aren't using rational thought…"

"Mason! Do you think I need coddling?" Draven shouted. "If you mean to be so damned helpful, go and clear the brush before me."

They trudged along in tense silence until they came to the clearing where their horses were still tied to the trees where they left them. Draven gave Mason a hard stare and handed him the girl while he mounted his horse and settled into the saddle. Silently he leaned down and took her from Mason, positioning her sideways in the saddle, keeping one arm around her to hold her in place as he held the reins with the other.

The last of their journey home they rode at a smooth canter, the girl resting limply against Draven's chest. She didn't turn to him or cuddle closer, instinctively seeking security as he had expected. She simply lay in his arms limply, her head bouncing softly against his shoulder. He held her frail body close to his. There was so little warmth in her and she seemed so weak.

She needed help but he was not unaware of the danger she presented. He felt something surrounding her, and from beyond her; something corrupt, something adverse. His frown deepened and his arm stiffened around her. She moaned but he didn't loosen his grip. Silently he offered prayer to Iybae for guidance and wisdom.

Why an electronic book?

We live in the Information Age—an exciting time in the history of human civilization in which technology rules supreme and continues to progress in leaps and bounds every minute of every hour of every day. For a multitude of reasons, more and more avid literary fans are opting to purchase e-books instead of paperbacks. The question to those not yet initiated to the world of electronic reading is simply: *why?*

1. *Price.* An electronic title at Ellora's Cave Publishing runs anywhere from 40-75% less than the cover price of the <u>exact same title</u> in paperback format. Why? Cold mathematics. It is less expensive to publish an e-book than it is to publish a paperback, so the savings are passed along to the consumer.

2. *Space.* Running out of room to house your paperback books? That is one worry you will never have with electronic novels. For a low one-time cost, you can purchase a handheld computer designed specifically for e-reading purposes. Many e-readers are larger than the average handheld, giving you plenty of screen room. Better yet, hundreds of titles can be stored within your new library—a single microchip. (Please note that Ellora's Cave does not endorse any specific brands. You can check our website at www.ellorascave.com

for customer recommendations we make available to new consumers.)

3. *Mobility.* Because your new library now consists of only a microchip, your entire cache of books can be taken with you wherever you go.

4. *Personal preferences are accounted for.* Are the words you are currently reading too small? Too large? Too…**ANNOYING**? Paperback books cannot be modified according to personal preferences, but e-books can.

5. *Innovation.* The way you read a book is not the only advancement the Information Age has gifted the literary community with. There is also the factor of what you can read. Ellora's Cave Publishing will be introducing a new line of interactive titles that are available in e-book format only.

6. *Instant gratification.* Is it the middle of the night and all the bookstores are closed? Are you tired of waiting days—sometimes weeks—for online and offline bookstores to ship the novels you bought? Ellora's Cave Publishing sells instantaneous downloads 24 hours a day, 7 days a week, 365 days a year. Our e-book delivery system is 100% automated, meaning your order is filled as soon as you pay for it.

Those are a few of the top reasons why electronic novels are displacing paperbacks for many an avid reader. As always, Ellora's Cave Publishing welcomes your questions and comments. We invite you to email us at service@ellorascave.com or write to us directly at: 1337 Commerce Drive, Suite 13, Stow OH 44224.